'Poppy.'

With a start she turned towards the sound of the deep but expressionless voice and instantly recognised those familiar and tormented eyes. Surprise was tinged with concern and her heart beat faster. 'Matt? I didn't exp... Are you all—?' But his taut face stole her words, silencing her.

Go for neutral. 'You finished up earlier than I did.'

With his mouth grim and tense, he strode straight to her, his hands gripping the tops of her arms. Silently, he hauled her up onto her toes, pulled her against him, and then took her mouth in a kiss, plundering it with a frenzy close to desperation.

Surprise spun through her at the fact he was even here, and intensified at the knowledge he still wanted her—given what had gone down in the ED. She opened her lips under his, wanting and trying to claim her place in the kiss and struggling to find it. She'd never been kissed quite like it: urgent need spinning together with what she guessed was misery.

With a gasp, he pulled his mouth away and, still silent, grabbed her hand, tugging her up the hallway to the bedroom. Her feet stumbled at the speed, and she should have been angry, perhaps even on one level scared, but all she could feel was his pain roaring through her like a hot wind.

Then his mouth was on hers again: hot, hard and frantic. And she was tumbling back onto the bed.

Dear Reader

Poppy Stanfield is a successful surgeon who's on the cusp of being made Chief of Surgery: her ultimate goal and everything she's spent years working towards. So when she's suddenly sent to Bundallagong not only does she think she has landed on Mars, she thinks life as she knows it has ended too. All she can see is plains and red dust, and not even the sparkling Indian Ocean is enough to win her over. From the first moment she steps onto Bundallagong soil she is making plans to leave.

But sometimes what we think is the worst thing possible turns out to be the best thing that ever happened to us. Poppy has no clue that this is going to be her story, and she's not quick to realise it either as she rails against everything Bundallagong throws at her.

Dr Matt Albright had the perfect life until it was stolen from him, and now he doesn't care where he lives or who lives with him—which is why he's totally ignoring the goanna that has moved into his roof! He goes to work each day and goes through the motions of living, hating that the town he loves now walks on eggshells around him. When he first meets Poppy all he can see is a starchy, uptight woman who is going to drive him absolutely spare.

The isolation of the Outback, with its fiery heat, will either send you mad or heal you; I'll let you read on to find out what is in store for Poppy and Matt! ☺

I hope you enjoy their story! For photos of the area that inspired the story, head to my website at www.fionalowe.com. I love to chat to my readers, and you can also find me at Facebook (Fiona Lowe author), Twitter and at eHarlequin's Medical Romance Authors' blog or via my website. I'd love to hear from you!

Happy reading!

Love

Fiona x

CAREER GIRL
IN THE COUNTRY

BY
FIONA LOWE

MILLS
BOON

Always an avid reader, **Fiona Lowe** decided to combine her love of romance with her interest in all things medical, so writing Medical™ Romance was an obvious choice! She lives in a seaside town in southern Australia, where she juggles writing, reading, working and raising two gorgeous sons with the support of her own real-life hero!

Recent books by the same author:

SINGLE DAD'S TRIPLE TROUBLE
THE MOST MAGICAL GIFT OF ALL
HER BROODING HEART SURGEON
MIRACLE: TWIN BABIES

To Sandra, with many thanks for keeping us neat and tidy!

CHAPTER ONE

FEMALE SURGEON TAKES BAMPTON AWARD

Ms Stanfield's meteoric rise in the male-dominated field of surgery was recognised last week. **Journal**'s 'on the ground' photographer snapped Ms Stanfield wearing last season's black suit (right), and we're left wondering if rather than taking the 'Old Boys' Club' by storm she's actually joined it. Rumour has it she's in negotiations with two prestigious hospitals for Chief of Surgery.

POPPY STANFIELD'S 6:00 a.m. sip of Saturday coffee turned bitter in her mouth as she read the five-line article on the back page of the Perth newspaper. She didn't give a damn about the bitchy comment on her cinch-waisted black suit but how the hell had the gossip columnist found out about the job interviews? One job interview especially—the one she'd very carefully and deliberately kept quiet because it was hard enough being female in this business, let alone having the temerity to want a top job. A top job she was determined to get one way or another, which was why she'd applied for the post of

Chief of Surgery at Southgate as well as Perth City, the hospital she currently worked for.

And now 'one way' was her only remaining option.

Her disappointed gaze caught sight of the envelope with the Southgate crest that had arrived yesterday containing a letter with the words 'unsuccessful candidate'. She hadn't read past them because there'd been no point. Poppy Stanfield didn't lose, she just regrouped and planned a new strategy. It would have been a huge coup to land the Southgate job ahead of the Perth City one, but the interview panel had been hostile from the moment she'd walked in.

The Bampton win had ruffled more than a few feathers in surgical ranks, and the media attention had been unexpected. The memory of the ditzy and pen-less journalist, with hair flying, who'd arrived late to interview her, sent a sliver of irritation down her spine. Poppy reread the article and the bald, incriminating words. Hell, why hadn't she spent more time with the journalist instead of rushing through the interview?

The faint echo of mocking laughter sounded deep down inside her. *You spend all your time at work and when have you ever really spent time with anyone?*

Steven.

Her phone chirped loudly, making her jump. Given it was 6:00 a.m., the call was most likely the hospital needing her for an urgent consult and absolutely nothing to do with this tiny article buried in the centre of the paper. Yes, an emergency consult would be the best scenario. The worst scenario would be— *Stop right there.* She refused to contemplate the worst scenario, but still she checked the screen before answering it.

She groaned into her hand. The name of the hospital's

executive medical officer and her current boss blinked at her in inky and unforgiving black. *Damage control.* Tilting her head back and bringing her chin up, she answered the call with a firm, crisp greeting. 'Hello, William.'

'Poppy.' The professor spoke her name as if it pained his tongue to roll over the combination of letters. 'I've just seen the paper.'

Show no weakness. 'You must be pleased.' She ignored the vividly clear picture of him in her mind—tight face and stern mouth—the way he always looked when he believed a staff member had let him down. She infused her voice with enthusiasm. 'It was an excellent article about your groundbreaking in utero surgery.'

'It was, and surprisingly accurate, but that's not the article I'm referring to.'

No way was she admitting to anything so she let the deliberate silence ride, biting her lip not to say a word.

William continued. 'In your thank-you speech at the Bampton awards you said you were committed to Perth City.'

She pushed the Southgate envelope under the paper and out of sight. 'Absolutely. City's given me every opportunity.' The words of her speech flowed out smoothly, in stark contrast to the reality, which had involved her fighting to get into the surgery programme, working harder and longer hours than her male counterparts and ignoring the advice that surgery took beautiful young women and turned them into ugly old ones. She'd stopped thinking of herself as a woman long ago and with it had gone the dream of marriage and a family of her own. 'Should the board see fit, it would be an honour to serve as the Chief of Surgery.'

'An honour?'

His tone bristled with sarcasm, which Poppy ignored. 'Yes, indeed, and as I outlined in my interview with the board, I can start immediately and provide a seamless transition period before Gareth leaves for Brisbane.'

'The board's still deliberating on the best person for the position.' His voice dripped with disapproval. 'But I'm reassured by your commitment to the hospital, and by knowing how much of an honour you consider it to be working for the WA Healthcare Network.'

She let go of a breath she hadn't realised she'd been holding. 'Excellent.'

'So it stands to reason that you were the *first* person we thought of when Bundallagong Hospital requested a visiting surgeon.'

'Excuse me?' Of all the possible things she might have anticipated him saying, that wasn't one of them.

'Bundallagong Hospital.' William repeated the name slowly, a hint of humour skating along the cool steel of his voice, as if he was party to a private joke.

Her brain stalled, trying to think why the name of the town was vaguely familiar, and with a start she frantically flicked the pages of the paper open until she found the weather map. Her gasp of surprise was too quick for her mouth to stifle. 'But that's fifteen hundred kilometres away!'

'Or nine hundred and thirty-two miles, which is why they need a visiting surgeon for three months.'

Years of well-honed control started to unravel. 'William, this is ridiculous. Sending me out into the boonies is only going to make the day-to-day running at City even tighter than it is.'

'We've allowed for that.'

Her stomach clenched at his terse tone. 'We've been chasing staff for over a year and what? Now you've just pulled a surgeon out of a hat?'

'One of the east coast applicants will fill your position while you're away.'

The staccato delivery of his words shot down the line like gunfire and she rocked back as if she'd been hit. The board was deliberately sending her away so they could observe her opposition in action without her being around to counteract any fallout. Incandescent fury flowed through her. 'And let me guess, that surgeon would be male.'

A sharp intake of breath sounded down the line. 'Poppy, you know I can't disclose information like that. Besides, as you've always pointed out, gender is irrelevant and it's all about expertise.'

He'd used her words against her to suit his own ends.

'Let's just be totally honest, shall we, William? You're seriously ticked off that I applied to Southgate and now you're punishing me for doing what any other surgeon in my position would have done.'

'Now you're being irrational, which isn't like you at all. Go to Bundallagong, Poppy, do your job and let the board do theirs. My secretary will be in touch about flight details but start packing because you're leaving tomorrow.'

The phone line suddenly buzzed and she realised he'd hung up on her. Blind anger tore through her and she shredded the newspaper, venting unprintable expletives at the journalist, William, the hospital and the system in general. Who the hell was this interloper from the east coast? She had contacts and she'd find out because learning about the enemy was a vital part of the strategy of winning.

But as the final strips of paper floated to the floor, her anger faded almost as fast as it had come and uncharacteristic tears of frustration and devastation pricked her eyes. Suddenly she was whipped back in time to when she had been a gangly ten-year-old girl valiantly trying to hold back tears after a drubbing in the first set of a tennis final, one of the few matches her father had actually turned up to watch.

He'd crossed his arms and stared down at her, his expression filled with derision. *'Don't be such a girl. Do you think boys cry? They don't. They just go out there and win.'*

Shaking her head as if that would get rid of the memory, she stomped into her bedroom and hauled a suitcase out of the wardrobe. If Bundallagong Hospital needed a surgeon then, by God, they were getting one, and the staff there wouldn't know what had hit them. She'd clear the waiting list, reorganise the department, overhaul the budget, meet every target and make William and the board sit up and take notice. Nobody put Poppy Stanfield in a corner.

Dr Matt Albright was on an island beach. The balmy tropical breeze skimmed over his sun-warmed skin and a book lay face-down on his naked chest, resting in the same position it had been for the last half-hour.

'Daddy, watch me!'

He waved to his daughter as she played in the shallow and virtually waveless water, then he rolled onto his side towards his wife, who lay next to him, reading.

At that precise moment he knew his life was perfect in every way.

She glanced up and smiled in her quiet and unassuming way.

He grinned. 'You do realise I've loved you from the moment you hit me with play dough at kinder.'

Her tinkling laughter circled him and he leaned in to kiss her, knowing her mouth as intimately as his own. He reached out to curve his hand around her shoulder, trying to pull her closer, but his fingers closed in on themselves, digging into his palm. He tried again, this time cupping her cheeks, but they vanished the moment he tried to touch them.

'Daddy!'

He turned towards his daughter's voice and saw her evaporating, along with the water that tore all the sand from the beach. Panic bubbled hot and hard in his veins and he sat up fast, hearing the sound of his voice screaming 'No!'

His eyes flew open into darkness, his heart thundering against his ribs and sweat pouring down his face. His hands gripped something so hard they ached and he realised his fingers were digging deep into the edge of the mattress. He wasn't on a beach.

He was in a bed.

Slowly his eyes focused and he recognised the silhouette of his wardrobe, and he heard the thumping and scratching of the goanna that had at some point in the last few months, without any protest from him, moved into the roof.

Bundallagong. He was in Bundallagong.

He fell back onto the pillow and stared blindly up at the ceiling. His heart rate slowed and the tightness in his chest eased and for one brief and blessed moment he felt nothing at all. Then the ever-present emptiness, which the dream had momentarily absorbed, rushed back in. It expanded wide and long, filling every crevice, every cell and tainting every single breath.

Sleep was over. He swung his legs out of bed, walked into the lounge room, stared out into the night, and waited for the dawn.

'And how long have you had this pain, Sam?' Poppy pulled the modesty sheet back over the young man's abdomen.

He shrugged. 'Dunno. I think I saw Dr Albright about a month ago but then it just went away.'

'And is today's pain worse than a month ago?'

'A lot.'

'The nurse tells me you've been vomiting?'

'Yeah, sorry about that.'

Poppy tried not to smile. Dressed in tough mining workwear, and looking like not even a bullet could take him down, Sam's politeness and air of bewilderment reminded her of a young boy rather than a strapping and fit man of twenty.

'I'll be back in a bit, Sam.' Poppy pulled the screen curtains shut behind her as she stepped out into the compact emergency department, running the symptoms through her head—fever, high white blood cell count, rebound tenderness and an ultrasound that showed nothing unusual, although that in itself wasn't unusual. The process of diagnosis soothed her like the action of a soothing balm and she relaxed into the feeling.

The shock of landing two hours ago on the Mars-scape that was Bundallagong still had her reeling. The green of the river-hugging suburbs of Perth had not prepared her for the barrenness of the Pilbara. When she'd exited the plane, her feet had stuck mutinously to the roll-away airport stairs as her gaze had taken in the flat, red dust plains that stretched to the horizon in three directions. Then the ferocious dripping heat had hit her like an impenetrable wall and it had been like walking into a raging furnace with an aftershock of wet, cloying steam. The irony wasn't lost on her—William had sent her to hell.

The only way to reduce her 'sentence' was to start work so she'd asked the taxi driver to take her directly to the hospital. The fact it was a Sunday afternoon mattered little because the sooner she started her rotation, the sooner she could finish. She'd planned to spend a couple of hours studying medical histories and drawing up her first week's surgical list but as she'd arrived, so had Sam. The nurse on duty had happily accepted her offer of help with a smile, saying, 'Thanks heaps. It'll give the on-call doctor a break.'

Now Poppy walked briskly to the nurses' station and dropped the history in front of Jen Smithers, whose badge read 'Nursing Administrator'. 'Sam's got appendicitis so if you can arrange everything, I'll meet him in Theatre in an hour.'

The nurse, who Poppy guessed was of a similar age to her, looked up, a startled expression on her face. 'So it's an emergency case?'

'Not strictly, but he'll be better off without his appendix and there's no time like the present.'

'Ah.' Jen spun a pen through her fingers, as if considering her thoughts.

Poppy rarely took no for an answer and the 'Ah'

sounded ominous. She made a snap decision: she needed the nursing staff on her side but she also needed to show she was the one in charge of the team. 'Jen, I call a spade a spade and I don't play games. I'll be straight with you and you need to be straight with me. I want to operate on Sam this afternoon and I expect you to do your job so I can do mine.'

Jen nodded, her demeanour friendly yet professional. 'Fair enough. I can get nursing staff in to staff Theatre and Recovery, but that isn't going to be enough. It's the anaesthetic registrar's weekend off and he's not due back from Bali until this evening's flight.'

Gobsmacked, Poppy stared at her, not knowing whether to be more stunned that a person could fly direct to Bali from the middle of nowhere or the fact that it left the town without an anaesthetist. 'Surely there's someone else?'

'Well, yes, technically there is, but...'

A tight band of tension burned behind Poppy's eyes. Hell, she really *had* come to Mars. She didn't have time for staff politics, especially if they got in the way of her doing her job and proving to William that she deserved the chief of surgery position back in Perth. 'Just ring the doctor and get him or her here, and leave the rest to me.'

Jen gave a wry smile. 'If you're sure, I can do that.'

'Of course, I'm sure.' Poppy headed back to her patient, shaking her head. It seemed a very odd thing to say but, then again, she was a long way from Perth. She busied herself inserting an IV into Sam's arm, administered Maxolon for his nausea and pethidine for the pain.

'This will have you feeling better soon.'

'Thanks, Doc.'

'No problem.'

She clicked her pen and started scrawling a drug order onto the chart when she heard voices coming from the direction of the nurses' station. She couldn't make out Jen's words but could hear her soft and conciliatory tone, followed quickly by a very terse, deep voice asking, 'Why didn't you call me first?'

'Because Ms Stanfield was here and I thought I could save you—'

As Poppy hung the chart on the end of the trolley, Jen's voice was cut off by the male voice. The anger was unmistakable and his words hit painfully hard. 'Save me? I don't need you or anyone else in this town making decisions for me, do you understand? I'm the on-call doctor today and that means I get called.'

Sam's head swung towards the raised voices, his expression full of interest.

Staff politics. She'd asked Jen to call in this guy so she needed to be the one to deal with him. 'Back in a minute, Sam.' Poppy grabbed the cubicle curtains and deliberately pulled them open with a jerk, making the hangers swish against the metal with a rushing ping to remind Jen and the unknown doctor that there was a patient in the department. She marched briskly to the desk.

'Oh, Ms Stanfield.' Jen glanced around the man standing with his back to Poppy. Her organised demeanour had slipped slightly but instead of looking angry or crushed at being spoken to as if she was a child, her expression was one of resignation tinged with sadness and regret. 'Poppy Stanfield, meet Dr. Matt Albright, Head of ED.'

The tall, broad-shouldered man turned slowly, his sun-streaked chestnut hair moving with him. It was longer than the average male doctor's and the style was either deliberately messy-chic or overdue for a cut. A few strands fell forward, masking his left cheek, but his right side was fully exposed, and olive skin hollowed slightly under a fine but high cheekbone before stretching over a perfectly chiselled nose. A dark five-o'clock shadow circled tightly compressed lips, leaving Poppy in no doubt of his masculinity.

With a jolting shock she realised he wasn't handsome—he was disconcertingly beautiful in a way that put everyone else into shadow. In ancient times he would have been sculpted in marble and raised onto a pedestal as the epitome of beauty. Poppy found herself staring as if she was in a gallery admiring a painting where the artist had created impossibly stunning good looks that didn't belong on battle-scarred earth.

He was heart-stoppingly gorgeous and she'd bet anything women fell at his feet. Once she would have too but thankfully, due to years of practice, she was now immune and not even a quiver of attraction moved inside her.

Nothing ever does any more.

Shut up. Work excites me. She extended her hand towards him. 'Matt.'

His hand gripped hers with a firm, brisk shake, and a faint tingling rush started, intensifying as it shot along her arm. *Immune, are you?*

Compressed nerve from a too-firm grip, that's all.

'Poppy.' He raised his espresso-brown eyes to meet her gaze. She expected to see at least a flicker of interest in a new colleague, almost certainly a calculating professional sizing-up, and, at worst, a derisive flare at the fact she was a surgeon and a woman. None of it worried her because she knew exactly how to handle the men she worked with—she'd had years of experience.

But what she saw was so unexpected that it sucked the air from her lungs, almost pulling her with it. A short, sharp flame flickered in his eyes for a split second, il-luminating hunger, but as it faded almost as fast as it had flared, she caught deep and dark swirling shadows before clouds rolled in briskly, masking all emotion.

She swayed on her heels as his hunger called up a blast of her own heat but as she glimpsed the misery in his eyes, she shivered and a jet of arctic cold scudded through her. Fire and ice collided; lust and pain coiling together before spiralling down to touch a place that had been firmly closed off and abandoned since—

She abruptly pulled her hand out of his, breaking his touch and moving her gaze to his left shoulder. *There you go, simple solution: no eye contact.* She didn't want to care about what hid behind that flawless face and now that his heat wasn't flowing through her, she marshalled her wayward thoughts and valiantly recomposed herself. This was no time to be discomfited. She needed to be in control and in charge, her future depended on it.

'As Jen will have explained, I need you to anaesthe-tise Sam Dennison.'

Long, lean fingers on his right hand crossed his wide and casually clad chest, flicking at the sleeve band of his white T-shirt. 'This is my department and I need to examine *my* patient before any decisions are made.' He turned and walked towards the cubicle.

Poppy matched his stride. 'And as Bundallagong's

resident surgeon for the next ninety days or less, it's my considered opinion that—'

'You've had time to examine Sam and now you need to extend that courtesy to me.'

He didn't alter his pace and before she could reply, Matt Albright stepped through the curtains and closed them in her face.

CHAPTER TWO

MATT could hear the new surgeon pacing, her black heels clicking an impatient rhythm against the linoleum floor. Well, she could just wait. He wasn't a stickler for protocol but Jen had overstepped the mark by not calling him in to examine Sam first. God, he was sick of the town walking on eggshells around him and trying to protect him when all he wanted was normality. *Yeah, and what exactly is that these days?*

'You OK, Doc?' The young miner lay propped up against a bank of pillows, his eyes slightly glazed from the opiate pain relief.

Hell, if a spaced-out patient noticed he was shaking with frustration then things were really spinning out.

Matt, how can you always be so calm? Lisa's slightly accusing voice sounded faintly in his head. But that conversation had taken place in another lifetime, before everything he'd held dear had been brutally stolen from him. He hadn't known calm in over a year.

'I'm fine.' *Pull the other one.* 'But you're not. That appendix rumbling again?'

'Yeah, although whatever that other doctor gave me is good stuff.' Sam grinned happily.

Matt smiled as he examined him. 'Have you got any family up here?'

Sam shook his head. 'Nah, came for the job and the money.'

'I'll arrange for a phone so you can talk to your mum because there's a very high chance you'll be parting with your appendix. We'll fast you from midnight and observe you overnight.'

'OK.'

'Any questions?'

'Nah, you explained it all last time and then it got better.' Sam's eyes fluttered closed as the drugs really kicked in, tempering any concern over the surgery that he might have.

Matt decided he'd explain it all again to him later. He pulled the curtains open and the new surgeon immediately ceased pacing, but she held her wide shoulders square and tight. It struck him that there was nothing soft about this woman except for her name.

And her mouth.

Guilt kicked him hard. His initial top-to-toe glance of her had stalled unexpectedly on her mouth and a flash of lust-filled heat had sparked momentarily, shocking him deeply. There'd only ever been *one* woman for him, and until ten minutes ago no one else had ever registered on his radar, let alone elicited such a response. But there'd been something about Poppy Stanfield's plump mouth that had held him mesmerised. Lips that peaked in an inviting bow were the colour of crushed strawberries and hinted at tasting like an explosion of seductive sweetness. He'd almost licked his own in response.

It was a totally ridiculous and over-the-top reaction given the contrast between the softness of the lips and the precise and no-nonsense words they formed. Everything else about Poppy Stanfield was sharp angles and harsh lines. Her long black hair was pulled straight back exposing a high and intelligent forehead. Black hair, black brows, black suit, black shoes; the monotone was only broken by her lush mouth and the most unexpectedly vivid blue eyes.

Eyes that were fixed on him, full of questions and backlit with steely determination.

He deliberately sat on the desk and put a foot up on a chair, the position screaming casual in stark contrast to her starchy demeanour. For some crazy reason he had to concentrate really hard to get her name correct because, apart from being the colour of her lips, Poppy didn't suit her at all.

Her fingers tugged sharply at the bottom of her suit jacket, which was ludicrously formal attire for Bundallagong, and she seemed to rise slightly on her toes so she wasn't much shorter than him. 'Dr Albright.'

'You're in the bush now, Poppy.'

Her gaze drifted to the red dust on his boots before moving up to his face. 'Oh, I'm *very* well aware of that.'

Her tone oozed urban superiority and for the first time in months something other than anger and despair penetrated his permanent sadness—the buzz of impending verbal sparring. No one had faced up to him or even questioned him since Lisa. Hell, half the time his friends and colleagues had trouble meeting his gaze and, like Jen, their well-meaning attempts to help only stifled him. But he had a citified stranger in front of him who knew nothing about him and he realised with unexpected relish that he was looking forward to this upcoming tussle.

He met Poppy's baby-blue eyes with a deadpan expression. 'Excellent. Oh, and by the way, we use first names here even when we're ticked off.'

Her eyes flashed but her mouth pursed as if she was working hard not to smile. It was the first sign that a sense of humour might lurk under all the superficial blackness.

'Thank you for that tip, *Matt*. So you agree with my diagnosis that Sam has appendicitis?'

'I do.' He tilted his head ever so slightly in acquiescence. He didn't have any problem with her diagnosis, just her modus operandi. 'The pain he was presented with last month has intensified.'

Poppy schooled her face not to show the sweet victory that spun inside her. 'So we're in agreement. He's been fasting due to his nausea so Jen can prep him for Theatre and—'

'I said I agreed with your diagnosis.' He raised one brow. 'That doesn't translate into agreeing with your treatment plan.'

The coolness of his tone didn't come close to soothing the hot and prickly frustration that bristled inside her, and she silently cursed William for sending her to the middle of nowhere where men ruled and women had no choice but to follow. 'So you're going to sit on it until his appendix bursts and we're faced with dealing with peritonitis?'

Emotionless molasses-coloured eyes bored into her. 'Not at all. He requires surgery and he'll have it—tomorrow.'

So this is a power play: my turf versus your turf. 'But

he could deteriorate overnight and we'd have to come in anyway. Tomorrow is an unknown quantity, whereas right now it's quiet, we're both here, so why wait?'

'Technically you don't even start work until 8:00 a.m. tomorrow.'

'That's semantics.'

He lowered his gaze and stared at her bright red suit-case stowed by the desk and then he moved the stare to her. 'Is it? It's Sunday and I would have thought seeing as you've only just arrived, you'd want to get settled in the house, hit the supermarket and fill your fridge.'

Something about his unflinching gaze made her feel like he saw not just the persona she showed the world but way beyond it and down deep into the depths she hadn't allowed anyone to enter since Steven.

But he really didn't want to—

I am so not doing this now!

She shut the voice up, hating that her hand had crept to the pendant that sat just below her throat. She forced her arm back by her side and her voice came out stiff and authoritative. 'You don't have to concern yourself with my domestic arrangements.'

'Very true.' He radiated a controlled aura that was an odd mix of dark and light, although the dark dominated. 'But I do concern myself with my staff's. They have lives outside work, Poppy.' His expression intimated that he thought perhaps she didn't. 'This is not an emergency and therefore we are *not* interrupting their family time, their fishing and sailing time, and, for some, their afternoon naps.'

'Afternoon naps?' Her voice rose in disbelief as her brain tried unsuccessfully to wrap itself around such a foreign concept. 'You're joking.'

Matt gave a snort that sounded like a rusty laugh as his face creased stiffly into lines that bracketed his mouth and for a moment his lips broke their tight line. A streak of something close to warmth followed, giving life and character to his face, which up until this point had been almost a caricature of unmarred features.

Her gut lurched as a flicker of delicious shimmers moved through her and she wished he'd stop. Perfection she could resist. Deep life lines around those dark and empty eyes, not so much.

His expression neutralised as the shadows returned. 'Life is slower here and, as you'll discover, the humidity at this time of year really saps your energy.'

She thought of the chief of surgery job back in Perth and went back into battle. She knew this game and she didn't plan to give an inch. 'Nothing saps my energy. I'm here to work, not to relax.' She reached for her briefcase and pulled out a folder. 'In regard to staff, I have a surgical budget and my own staffing ratios, and it's my call when to operate, not yours.'

'It is, and come tomorrow, your first official day, when David, the anaesthetic registrar, is back on duty, you can order him about to your heart's content. Today, as the ED doctor and the back-up anaesthetist, it's my call. We're not operating on Sam just so you can rush in, set a precedent and get some runs on the board.'

'This has *nothing* to do with me and everything to do with patient care.' She protested too quickly as his words hit far too close to home. Sam's case technically wasn't an emergency but it wasn't strictly elective surgery either. She hated that he'd guessed at her need to operate so she could stake her claim as the incumbent surgeon, competent and in charge.

He slid to his feet, the movement as graceful as a gazelle's but with the calculation of a panther. Everything about him screamed, *I don't believe you.*

'Should Sam's condition change, I'll call you straight away. Meanwhile, go stock your fridge and turn on the air-conditioning so you can sleep tonight.'

Her body vibrated with rage. 'Don't patronise me.'

Genuine surprise raced across his face and he gave a sigh filled with fatigue. 'I'm not. I'm actually trying to help. Your life here will be a lot easier if you don't get the staff off-side before you've officially started.'

She wanted to stay furious with him, she wanted to cast him in the role of obstructive male, but his gaze wasn't combative and amid the darkness that hovered around him, she detected a sliver of goodwill. It totally confused her.

'I see. Well, we may not agree about Sam but I take on board what you're saying.' She made herself say, 'Thank you.'

'No problem.' His fingers pushed through his straight hair, the strands sliding over them like water on rocks.

With a shock she caught the glint of gold on his ring finger. How had she missed that? But it didn't matter how or why—what was important was now she knew. Married men didn't interest her.

It's been a long time since an unmarried one interested you.

Get off my case!

She had a gut feeling that she and Matt Albright would probably spend the next ninety days disagreeing but now it would be without fear of those strange and unwanted shimmers. Working with Matt would be uncomplicated and all about the job, and that was what she did best.

She pulled out a business card and held it towards him.

'This is my mobile number should Sam deteriorate, and meanwhile I'll let you get back to your Sunday afternoon and your family.'

The goodwill vanished from his eyes as his lean body ceased all movement, and an eerie stillness hovered around him.

So much for her attempt at being polite. She couldn't work him out.

The card hung between them for a moment and then he slowly raised his arm and plucked it from her fingers. 'Right. See you around.'

'I guess you will.' What else was there to say?

'Wait!' Jen hurried over as two bloodied men supported and half dragged another man into the department.

'What happened?' Matt hauled his way back from the black despair Poppy's innocent comment had plunged him into, hating that it had, and was glad to be able to focus on the patient.

'Patient involved in a brawl, suspected head injury and possible fractures.'

He grabbed a gown and stifled a groan. In years gone by, drunken brawls had been exclusively Saturday night's domain but the mining boom had brought more people into the town and some of them had more money than sense. This patient could have anything from a broken toe to a subdural haematoma, with a million possibilities in between.

He threw Poppy a gown. 'I think you just got a

reprieve from filling your fridge but just so we're clear, this is my emergency and you're assisting.'

'Oh, absolutely.' But deep sapphire blue shards scudded across her enormous baby-blue eyes, making a mockery of her supposed compliance. 'It's your emergency right up to the point when you realise he needs surgery and you're totally out of your depth.'

No one had been that blunt with him in a long time. A noise rumbled up from deep down inside him and for a moment he didn't recognise the sound. With a shock of surprise he realised that for the first time in months he'd just laughed.

Matt moved into action, work being one of the few things in his life he didn't question. He called out to the two men, 'Help me get him onto this trolley.'

They half hauled and half dropped the injured man onto the mattress and as soon as the sides had been pulled up, Matt asked, 'Do either of you have any injuries or is that your mate's blood?'

'We're OK.'

Matt wasn't convinced. 'Sit over there and wait. As soon as we've checked out your mate, someone will examine you both. No one is to leave until you've been examined, do you understand?'

Both men looked sheepish. 'Yeah, Doc.'

He pushed the trolley into the resus room. 'What's his pulse ox?'

Poppy slid the peg-like device onto the end of the patient's finger. 'Eight-five.' She unravelled green plastic tubing and turned on the oxygen. 'Mr…?'

'Daryl Jameson.' Jen supplied the information.

'Mr Jameson. I'm Poppy Stanfield, this is Jen Smithers, and on your left is Dr Matt Albright. You're in good hands. We're just going to give you some oxygen and help you to sit up.'

Matt tried not to show his surprise that Poppy had failed to mention her qualifications and that unlike many surgeons she was actually quite personable with an awake patient. 'Daryl, how's the breathing, mate?'

'Hurts.'

'Where does it hurt?' Poppy adjusted the elastic to hold the nasal prongs in place.

'It's me chest and arm that's killing me.'

'Do you know what day it is?' Matt flicked on his penlight.

'Sunday. I remember everything up to the moment the idiot hit me.'

Matt flashed the light into his patient's eyes. 'Pupils equal and reacting.'

Jen tried to ease Daryl's shirt off but resorted to scissors when Daryl couldn't move his arm without flinching. The soft material separated, revealing purple bruising all over the thin man's chest. The nurse gasped.

Matt looked up from the IV he was inserting, hating that he knew exactly what would have caused such trauma. 'Steel-capped boots. Welcome to the seedier side of Bundallagong, Poppy.'

She attached electrodes to Daryl's chest, and at the same time Matt knew she was examining the rise and fall of his chest given the complaint about pain on breathing. 'Sinus tachycardia. Jen, organise for a chest and arm X-ray.'

'On it.' The nurse started to manoeuvre the portable X-ray machine into position.

While Poppy wrapped a blood-pressure cuff around their patient's uninjured arm to enable automatic readings, Matt swung his stethoscope into his ears and listened to Daryl's breathing. He could hear creps and he palpated a paradoxical movement of the chest wall. 'Flail chest. I'll insert prophylactic chest tubes.'

A frown furrowed her smooth, white brow. 'Good idea but it's the damage under the fractured ribs that worries me.'

Matt nodded. 'We're in agreement, then.'

'There's a first time for everything.'

The words sounded precise and clipped, but her plump, berry-red lips twitched. Like the siren's call, he felt his gaze tugged towards them again and wondered what they'd feel like to kiss.

The blood-pressure machine beeped loudly, ripping into his traitorous thoughts and grounding him instantly. He pulled his shame-ridden gaze away, reminding himself that he loved Lisa and he had a patient who needed his total concentration. 'Pressure's dropping.'

'He's bleeding somewhere.' Poppy's hands went direct to Daryl's abdomen, her alabaster fingers, with their neatly trimmed nails devoid of polish, palpating expertly. 'Any pain here?'

Daryl barely managed a negative movement of his head.

'No guarding. It's not his abdomen.' Poppy's frown deepened, making a sharp V between her expressive black brows. 'His O2 sats aren't improving. What about a haemothorax?'

'If he does have that, it's not massive because there's no mediastinal shift or tracheal deviation.'

But the blood-pressure machine kept beeping out its worrying sound as Daryl's heart rate soared and his conscious state started to fade. Matt stared at the green lines racing across the screen. PQRST waves scrawled the heartbeat but he thought he saw something unusual. He hit the printout button and studied the paper strips, detecting a change in the ST segment. Combining it with Poppy's musings, he had a sudden idea. 'Check his jugular vein.'

Matt shoved his stethoscope back in his ears and listened carefully to Daryl's heart beat. Instead of a loud and clear lub-dub, the sound was muffled.

'Cardiac tamponade.'

They spoke in unison, their thoughts and words meshing together for the very first time. 'He's bleeding into the pericardial sac.'

Poppy ran the ultrasound doppler over his chest, locating the heart. 'There you go.' She pointed to the dark shadow around the heart that squeezed the vital muscle.

Matt snapped on gloves and primed a syringe, knowing exactly what he had to do. Under ultrasound guidance, he withdrew the fluid from around the heart. 'Hopefully that will stabilise him until you work your magic.'

Her teeth scraped quickly over her bottom lip; the slightest of hesitations. 'A pericardial sac repair without the back-up of bypass isn't quite what I'd expected.'

He understood her concerns and he had some of his own. 'The anaesthetic will stretch me too.'

'It's going to be touch and go.'

'I know.' He met her direct and steady gaze, one devoid of any grandstanding or combative qualities, and wondered not for the first time about the many facets of Ms Poppy Stanfield.

CHAPTER THREE

IT HAD been a hell of a piece of theatre. Matt couldn't help but be impressed by Poppy's expertise. Except for requests for unanticipated instruments, she'd been virtually silent throughout, but it hadn't been an icy silence that had put the staff on tenterhooks; the case had done that on its own. Given the complexity of the surgery, she'd done the repair in a remarkably short space of time, giving Daryl the best chance of survival. It had been a lesson to Matt that she knew her stuff and did it well. Although many visiting surgeons had her air of authority, not all of them had the skills to match.

It had been one of the most challenging anaesthetics he'd ever given due to the patient being haemodynamically unstable, and maintaining his pressure had been a constant battle. Thankfully, Daryl had survived the emergency surgery and was now ventilated and on his way to Perth.

Once the flying doctor's plane had taken off and the night shift had arrived, Matt no longer had a reason to stay at the hospital. As he took the long way home it occurred to him that even Poppy had left the hospital before him, finally taking with her those bright red cases that matched her lips.

Again, shame washed through him. He hated it that he kept thinking about her bee-stung lips. He didn't want to because they belonged to a woman who was so different in *every* way from his wife that it didn't warrant thinking about. When he thought of Lisa the words 'fair, soft and gentle' came to mind. Poppy Stanfield wouldn't understand the description.

He pulled into his carport and as he reluctantly walked towards the dark and empty house, memories of past homecomings assailed him.

'Tough case, honey?'

'Yeah.'

'Well, you're home now.' Lisa leaned in to kiss him. *'Annie's already in bed and our room is deliciously cool.'*

His key hit the lock and the door swung open, releasing trapped and cloying heat, which carried silence with it in stark contrast to the past. God, he hated coming back to this house now.

Yeah, well, you hated not living in it.

He dropped his keys in a dish he'd brought home from the Pacific and which now sat permanently on the hall table, and thought about the months he'd stayed away from Bundallagong. Being back hurt as much as being away.

He turned the air-conditioner onto high, poured himself iced water and briefly contemplated going to bed. Picking up the remote, he turned on the television, rationalising that if he was going to stare at the ceiling he'd be better off staring at a screen. He flicked through the channels, unable to settle on watching anything that involved a story and eventually stared mindlessly at motor racing, the noise of the vehicles slowly lulling him into a soporific stupor.

He was back on the beach again, with dry heat warming his skin and coconut palms swaying in the breeze, a peaceful idyll that promised so much. Set back from the sand line was a grass hut, its roof thatched with dried sugarcane leaves, and he strode towards it quickly, anticipation humming through his veins. His family was waiting for him. He stepped up onto the lanai but instead of cane chairs there was a stretcher. Bewildered, he stepped over it and walked into the fale, expecting to see the daybed, but instead he was in an operating theatre that looked like a set from *MASH*, with patients lined up row upon row, some with sheets pulled over their heads. Voices shouted but he didn't recognise the words, and he turned back, wanting to run, but the lanai had vanished, leaving splintered timber as the only evidence of its existence.

Deafening noise roared and his arms came up to protect his head and then his eyes were suddenly open and the television was blaring out so loudly the walls vibrated. He must have rolled on the remote, taking the volume to full blast, and he quickly pumped it back to a bearable level, but the ringing in his ears took a moment to fade. He shook his head, trying to get rid of the buzzing, and thought perhaps bed was a better option than the couch—not that he wanted to sleep because the dreams would terrorise him.

As he swung his feet to the floor, a woman's scream curdled his blood. He quickly shoved his feet into his shoes, grabbed a torch and ran outside.

He heard a wire door slam and he moved his torch round to the house on his left, the house owned by the hospital. With a start he saw a tall, barefoot woman dressed in a long T-shirt standing on the steps, her arms wrapped tightly around her.

He jogged over as the outside lamp cast her in a pool of yellow light. 'Poppy? What the hell happened? Are you all right?'

She shuddered, her height seeming slightly diminished. She swallowed and it was if she had to force her throat to work. 'Mice.'

He knew his expression would be incredulous. The woman who'd stormed into his department with an approach similar to a man marking his territory had been reduced to a trembling mess by a mouse. For months he hadn't been able to laugh and now he had to try hard not to. '*You're* scared of a mouse or two?'

Her head flew up and a flash of the 'take no prisoners' woman he'd met nine hours ago surfaced. 'Not generally, no. But I opened the wardrobe to hang up my clothes and *mice* streamed out, scurrying over my feet, into my case and...' She took a steadying breath. 'I defy anyone, male or female, not to let out a yell of surprise when confronted by fifty of them.'

His mouth curved upwards, surprising muscles stiff from lack of use. 'That has to be an exaggeration of about forty-eight. Are they in the kitchen too?'

'I don't know!' Her voice snapped. 'I didn't stop to enquire if they'd taken over in there as well.'

Don't get involved. But he couldn't resist a dig. 'I did suggest you settle in to the house earlier in the day.'

Her chin shot up and she gave him a withering look. 'I am *not* exaggerating, and if that is the extent of your useful advice then I suggest you shut up now and leave.'

She crossed her arms and he suddenly noticed she had breasts. Small but round and… He hauled his gaze away. 'It's been a few months since anyone's lived here, although I would have thought someone would've checked out the house before you arrived. Who did you talk to in Administration?'

She stepped back inside, her gaze darting left and right and her long legs moving gingerly. 'No one.'

He followed. 'No one?' Usually Julie was very efficient.

'Me coming up here was—' She stopped abruptly for a moment. 'I rushed up here because the town was desperate. The fax telling you I was coming probably only arrived a few hours before me.'

They'd been desperate for weeks so her hasty arrival without the usual planning didn't make a lot of sense and he was about to ask her about it when a mouse raced out from under the couch.

Poppy leapt into the air, her long T-shirt rising up to expose creamy white thighs.

Matt tried not to look and instead marched like a foot soldier on patrol, punching open the kitchen door. Every surface was covered in mouse scats.

He heard Poppy's shocked gasp from the doorway but by the time he'd turned, her face was the usual mask of control, although she had a slight tremble about her.

'Just fabulous. This really is the icing on the cake of a stellar few days, and yet the poets wax lyrical about the bush.'

A startling fragility hovered around her eyes despite her sarcasm and he had an unexpected moment of feeling sorry for her. He shrugged it away. 'Living with a few creepy-crawlies is all part of the Bundallagong allure.'

'Not from where I'm standing it isn't. I think we have definition conflict on the word "few".'

Again he found himself wanting to smile yet at the same time a feeling of extreme restlessness dragged at him. He flung open cupboards and found mice squeaking and scurrying everywhere amidst bags of pasta, cereal, oats and biscuits, all of which had been chewed and their contents scattered. He slammed the doors shut. 'OK, you were right. It's a plague and with this many mice it probably means you don't have a python.'

Her eyes widened like the ongoing expanse of Outback sky and her hands flew to her hips. 'No snake? And *that's* supposed to make me feel better? Hell, and they give surgeons a bad rap about their bedside manner.'

This time the urge to smile won. 'Actually, a python would have meant fewer mice. I haven't seen an infestation like this in years. Your predecessor must have left food and I guess the cleaners figured it was nonperishable and left it for the next occupant. Thing is, time marched on and the mice moved in. Julie can get the exterminator to come in the morning.'

'The morning.' The words came out as a choked wail loaded with realisation. Another mouse shot past her and she stiffened for a second before hastily retreating to the lounge room.

Matt crossed the kitchen and leaned against the architrave, watching her. She had her back to him and was standing on tiptoe, reducing her contact with the floor to the bare minimum. One hand tugged at the base of the T-shirt in an attempt to make it longer, and the other pressed her mobile phone to her ear as she spoke briskly.

'Yes, I need the number for motels in Bundallagong. I don't have a pen so can you put me through direct?'

He thought about the suit she'd worn when they'd met and how it had been followed by surgical scrubs. Both garments had given her a unisex look, but the baggy shirt she wore now hid little. Poppy Stanfield might sound like a general but she had the seductive curves of a woman.

Heat hit him, making him hard, followed immediately by a torrent of gut-wrenching guilt. He loved Lisa. No woman could match her but for some reason his body had disconnected from his brain and was busy having a lust-fest. He hated it and every part of him wanted to get the hell out of the house and away from Poppy Stanfield and that damn T-shirt. But he couldn't leave, not until he knew she was settled in a motel. So he moved instead, putting distance between them by crossing the room and tugging his gaze away from the sweet curve of her behind that swelled out the T so beautifully that his palm itched.

He stared at the blank walls and then at the couch with a ferocious intensity he'd never before given to decor. He noticed a significant-size hole in the material covering the couch and realised the inside was probably full of rodents too. It would take days before baits and traps took effect, making the house liveable again.

He started making plans in his head to keep his mind off those long, shapely legs. As soon as he knew which motel she'd got a room at, he'd set the GPS in the hospital vehicle for her so she wouldn't get lost at this late hour. There'd be no point driving her because she'd need the car to get to and from the hospital.

Yeah, that, and you don't want to be in a car alone with her.

Poppy's voice suddenly went silent and the next moment, with a frustrated yell, she hurled her phone with a great deal of feeling onto the soft cushions of the couch. It was her first display of 'surgical temper'.

The outburst—so very different from Lisa's quiet approach—made him feel less guilty about getting hard, and yet it was so full of energy and life that it swirled around him, both pulling him in and pushing him away. After months of not feeling anything this maelstrom of emotions confused and scared him, and when he spoke, the words shot out harsh and loud. 'No instruments to throw?'

She didn't even raise a killing look. 'I have *never* thrown anything in Theatre, although I did train with a master thrower and once had to dodge a chair.' She plonked herself down hard on the couch, threw her head back and closed her eyes. 'This is a nightmare.'

Grey shadows hovered under her eyes and she looked exhausted.

'Actually, it's probably not a good idea to sit on that.' He pointed to the gnawed hole.

He'd expected her to fly off the couch but she merely shuddered and stayed put. Eventually she opened one eye and stared accusingly at him. 'You could have told me that the Australian billfish competition is on!'

Was it? Had that many months passed? 'Sorry, I didn't realise it was that time of year.' Once he'd had his finger on the pulse of his hometown and been part of the committee for one of the biggest events on the calendar, but not any more. Now days just rolled together into one long and empty period of time.

She frowned at him as if she didn't quite believe him. 'Every motel between here and a hundred k up and down the coast is fully booked out with anglers hoping to catch a two-hundred-and-twenty-kilo marlin. God, I hate this dust-impregnated town.' She picked up her phone and stared at it as if willing it to ring with news of a bed.

A mouse scuttled between his feet.

She can't stay here.

She's not staying with me.

Why not? You don't care about much any more so why care if she stays a few nights?

She sighed. 'I don't suppose you know if my office at the hospital has a couch?'

Her tone was unexpectedly flat, as if all the fight had gone out of her, and a tiny crack appeared in the blackness of his soul. His mouth started to work before his brain had fully thought it through. 'You can stay at my place until this joint is clean and mouse-free.'

Her smooth brow creased in uncertainty. 'That's kind of you but don't you think you should discuss it with your wife first?'

Your wife. He felt the darkness sucking at his heart and soul, threatening to drown him over again the way it had so many times in the last year and a half. His heart thumped faster, pumping pain with every beat, but he somehow managed to growl out, 'No need. Come on, grab your stuff. It's late.'

He turned and strode out of the house, not waiting for her, not offering to carry her case, and not looking back because if he did he might just change his mind. Not even Poppy deserved that.

* * *

Poppy lugged her unopened and mouse-free case the short distance to what she assumed was Matt's house—lights on, front door open—and wondered what on earth this man's deal was. He lurched from sarcastic to ironic, friendly to downright rude and a thousand emotions in between. Why offer her a bed if he clearly wasn't happy about her staying? She assumed he'd gone on ahead to let his wife know they had an unexpected guest. She thought of her gorgeous apartment in south Perth with a view of the river and silently cursed William and the hospital board.

She stepped into the empty foyer of a house considerably larger than her hospital residence, and unlike the minimalist furnishing of rental accommodation she could see the hand of a woman in the decor. Silence hovered and given it was close to midnight she didn't want to call out and wake anyone. For all she knew, there could be children asleep.

A closed door on her left was probably a bedroom so she left her case by the front door and padded down the well-lit hall, which opened into a formal lounge-dining area. Despite its stylish couches and polished wood table, it had an air of 'display only', lacking the personal touches like ornaments or photos that created living spaces. She kept walking and passed through a doorway into another huge space, which wasn't well-lit but she made out a kitchen and assumed beyond was a family room and bedrooms.

She spoke softly. 'Matt?'

He appeared through a door off the kitchen, his arms full of bed linen and his face set in unforgiving lines. 'Your room's this way.'

She expected him to turn towards the yet unexplored part of the house but instead he headed back from where she'd come from and entered the bedroom at the front of the house. A stripped white-wood queen-size bed dominated the room, which had a feature wall wallpapered in alternating cool blue and white stripes. Matching white-wood bedside tables held reading lamps with gold stands and white shades, although Poppy noticed the plugs had been pulled from the sockets. No books or boxes of tissues adorned any surfaces but gauzy curtains hung softly in front of a white blind, which was pulled down. The room should have said, 'restful haven for adults' but instead it looked abandoned.

Matt threw out the bottom sheet and Poppy moved to grab her side. She was almost certain this room had been designed to be the master bedroom. 'Are you sure this is OK?'

Matt deftly made a hospital corner with the top sheet and didn't meet her gaze. 'The en suite and walk-in wardrobe is through there.' He waved towards a doorway. 'The hot water's solar and it's really hot but it takes a minute or so to come through. Catch the water in the bucket unless you like to wake up to a cold shower.' He shoved a pillow so hard into the pillowcase it bunched up and he had to thump the feathers back into place before throwing it on the bed.

He strode to the door, his hand gripping the handle and his gaze fixed firmly on the cornice where two walls met. 'We leave at 7:30 a.m. and you'll find something for breakfast in the kitchen. Good night.'

The door closed firmly behind him, the click loudly stating, 'this is your space so stay here.' Poppy fell back onto the bed, her relief at being out of the infested house short-lived, and she wondered if she'd have been safer sharing with the mice.

Perhaps it had been sheer exhaustion but, despite Poppy's misgivings, she'd slept soundly. Now, as she dressed, she could feel the temperature climbing despite the early hour and her suit, which she donned automatically, felt hot. Still, if she had her way she'd be in scrubs soon enough. She opened her door, expecting to hear a household in full Monday morning action mode—radio or television news blaring, the drone of a kettle as it neared boiling and the ping of the toaster—but although she could hear the harsh squawk of cockatoos outside, she couldn't hear anything much inside. She made her way to the kitchen, which was empty, but with morning light streaming in she saw that, unlike the front part of the house, which held an unlived-in air, the kitchen showed more than the occasional sign of occupation.

Newspapers were piled so high on one end of the long granite bench that they'd started to slide onto the floor. Used cups and glasses sat abandoned close to, but not in, the dishwasher. A supermarket bag filled with tins took up more space rather than being stored in the adjacent pantry and every other surface was covered in clutter from half-opened mail to nails and paperclips.

A casual eating area off to the left had a table and chairs but instead of the polished jarrah having placemats it held a laptop and was covered in screeds of paper. She glanced into the family room and saw a similar chaotic mess that jarred with the decor, which had obviously been undertaken with care and a great eye for detail. Poppy wasn't a domestic queen by any stretch of the imagination but even she managed better than this. She was amazed the Albrights didn't have mice!

She filled the kettle and while she waited for it to boil for her heart-starter morning cup of coffee, she emptied the dishwasher, guessing where items went, and then reloaded it with the dirty cups and glasses. She located the coffee and then opened the fridge. Milk, a loaf of bread, three apples and a tub of yoghurt hardly made a dent in the cavernous space that was big enough to store food for a family of six.

'Morning.'

His voice startled her but at the same time it reminded her of a Cabernet Merlot from Margaret River: deep, complex and with a hint of tannin. She turned around and stifled a gasp as her body betrayed her with a shot of delicious, tingling lust.

He stood on the other side of the bench, his hair still slightly damp and rumpled from the shower, the ends brushing the collar of his open-necked shirt. His long fingers tackled the last few buttons and his tanned and toned chest fast disappeared under the placket. His wedding ring glinted in the sunshine through the window and when he raised his gaze, the Kelly green in his shirt lightened his dark eyes but the shadows remained, and fatigue hung over him like a threatening cloud.

What are you doing? Get yourself under control; he's married, off limits, and even if he wasn't he's too damn moody and you've sworn off men for all time.

The moody man spoke. 'Did you sleep?'

His question sounded almost accusatory. 'I did, thank you.' *But you don't look like you did.*

He seemed to be staring at her suit and she thought she detected relief in his eyes, which made no sense

whatsoever so she was probably totally wrong. She had
no clue why she was letting Matt Albright unnerve her.
If anyone unnerved her it was usually other women.
Men she understood because she worked in a man's
world but the whole women and friendship thing she'd
always found challenging and unfathomable, and that
dated back to primary school.

You're conveniently forgetting Steven, are you?

He didn't unnerve me, he just broke my heart.

And now you avoid men.

I work with men all the time!

That's not what I mean and you know it.

To distract herself she picked up a cloth and started
to wipe down the bench. 'No one else up yet?'

'You don't have to do that.' He swooped, his fingers brushing her skin as he tugged the cloth out of her
hand.

Trails of desire shot through her. This was crazy on
so many levels and she had to act. 'Look, Matt, I'm sorry
I had to prevail on your family for a bed, although you
were the one who offered. Obviously me being here is
a problem and I'd like to apologise to your wife for the
inconvenience.'

He lowered the dishcloth onto the sink, the action
slow and deliberate. When he raised his head she experienced a chill.

'My wife isn't here.'

*And you're an incredibly gorgeous guy that women
viscerally react to even when they're sensible and know
they shouldn't.* 'And she's not OK with me being here.
I get it.'

He grimaced. 'No, you don't get it at all, Poppy.' The
ping of the kettle sounded bright and cheery, in sharp

contrast to the strain in his voice and the emptiness in his eyes. 'She died.'

His grief rocked through her, sending out waves of shocked surprise, and her fingers immediately crept to the pendant at her neck. *Death*. She hadn't expected that. Suddenly everything fell into place: the vacant master bedroom; the messy kitchen; Jenny's lack of anger towards him yesterday; and his aura of immense sadness. 'I'm sorry. I shouldn't be here. I'll find somewhere else today.'

He scooped ground coffee beans into the plunger and dashed the hot water over them. 'It makes no difference to me if you stay or not.'

And she realised he spoke the truth. His perfectly handsome face that could have graced the cover of any magazine was a façade. Underneath it, pain burned inside him, making caring for anything difficult.

You should leave. 'When does the billfish thing finish?'

He consulted a wall calendar that was two months out of date, and turned the pages. 'Next Sunday. Everything will be booked solid until then.'

Hope sank in her gut like a lead weight. 'That's probably how long it will take them to get the house under control.'

'Could be.'

'So you're saying it's a waste of time even trying to find somewhere else?'

He shrugged as his hand closed around the coffee-pot. 'It's your call.' Lifting two clean mugs from the cupboard, he poured the coffee and held up the milk carton.

She shook her head at the milk and reached over,

lifting the black ambrosia to her nose, and breathed in deeply. The aroma sparked up her synapses, firing her brain into action. Was it such a bad thing if she had to stay here? She'd be working long hours so she'd hardly be in the house and when she was, she had her own room and bathroom so they'd hardly have to see each other. She had no doubt in her mind that Matt Albright was still very much struggling with the death of his wife so her occasional errant feelings, which she was certain she could squash, wouldn't be reciprocated at all, leaving everything as it should be: colleagues only.

'I came to operate, not to spend time trying to find a room, so, thanks, I'll stay.'

His blank expression and lack of response reinforced her decision and she brought the mug to her mouth, closed her eyes and drank in the brew. With a sigh of bliss she licked her lips and savoured every drop. She finally opened her eyes to find Matt's *chocolat-noir* gaze fixed intensely on her mouth and a spark of something broke through their blackness.

A shot of heat way beyond the definition of delicious tingling, and fully loaded with longing, rocked through her so hard and fast her knees sagged.

Get out now. 'I better get to the hospital and meet my staff.'

He gave a curt nod as the shadows scudded back in place. 'Don't give 'em hell.'

She bristled. 'I'll give them what they need.'

'I imagine you will.' His tone held resignation but his mouth curved slightly and the hint of dimple hovered in the darkness of his stubble, foreshadowing how heart-stoppingly magnificent he'd look wearing a full smile.

Poppy fled.

CHAPTER FOUR

POPPY flicked the switch on her Dictaphone to Off, having finished her last surgical report for the day. Her first couple of official workdays had arranged themselves into a routine of rounds, surgery, reports, phone calls to her spies in Perth to get an update on her opposition, and then arriving back at the house very late and falling exhausted into bed. Work consumed her, as it always did, only this time she appreciated that it left no space in her brain; no space to think about the way her body had gone into sensual overload when Matt Albright had looked at her through his heavy-lidded eyes.

She rubbed her forehead and wondered what on earth was wrong with her. Sure, he extended the handsome scale by about ten numbers but he was grumpy and short with everyone except patients, and obviously still grieving for his dead wife. Just like her, he wasn't fit for a relationship and she surely didn't even want one so there was absolutely *no* reason for her to be even thinking about him.

So why did thoughts of him sneak under her guard at random moments in the day? It made no sense and many times she'd needed to shake herself back into full-focus work mode because she had far more important things to think about, like the chief of surgery position in Perth.

'Ready, Poppy?'

The words broke into her thoughts and she glanced up, expecting to be asked for an emergency consult. Instead, Jen stood in the doorway dressed in casual clothes. 'Um, ready for what, exactly?'

Jen grinned. 'All work makes Poppy a dull girl.'

She straightened a pile of folders on her desk. 'All work is what I'm here to do.'

'Sure, but day is done and there's drinks at the pub.'

'Thanks but I'll pass.' Making small talk wasn't something that came easily to her; in fact, she was shockingly bad at it.

The nurse shook her head. 'Not an option, Poppy. It's a Bundallagong tradition that the nurses buy new medical staff a drink.'

She must have looked horrified because Jen hurriedly continued on with, 'Think of it as a girls' night out and a way of getting all the goss on the place.'

Her horror intensified. Poppy had no clue what a girls' night out entailed, having never been on one. *Getting the goss.* The words pierced her horror and she realised with a buzz of clarity that this might just be the solution to her problem of random thoughts about Matt interrupting her concentration. It was a normal human reaction to have natural curiosity when you heard unexpected news; healthy even, and Matt's statement about his wife being dead had been totally unexpected. She was pretty certain Matt wouldn't tell her any details and although she was known for her brusque, straight-shooting style, asking someone 'When and why did your wife die?' wasn't something even she would do. But if she found out the story from Jen then knowing would end the curiosity and banish all her unsettling feelings.

Decision made, she stood up, slung her handbag over her shoulder and joined Jen in the corridor. 'So how far away is the pub?'

'Next door.'

'There's a pub next to the hospital?' She couldn't hide her incredulity. 'Why haven't I seen it?'

'Its position is historical. Mining towns back in the day were pretty rough and I guess putting the two together was a short walk for the drunks. Today things are more PC so there's limited signage advertising the pub. It's mostly used by the hospital and college staff, so a fun crowd but not too rowdy.'

They stepped outside into the dusk and the ever-present heat enveloped them. Streaks of vermillion slashed the sky as the sun sank low against the horizon and the bright white light of the first star pierced the rising darkness. 'This sunset belongs on a postcard.'

'Yeah, it does from this direction, but turn one-eighty degrees and the port's infrastructure gets in the way. Mining dominates everything but I guess without it the town wouldn't exist.'

The sunset unexpectedly mellowed Poppy. 'Does the pub have a garden? Now you've planted the idea of a drink, a glass of champagne while watching this sunset might go down very well.'

Jen roared laughing. 'You can have any drink you like as long as it's beer or rum and Coke. Welcome to the north-west.'

The pub was busy and Jen made a bee-line for a table with a banquette seat on one side that had a reserved sign on it. The waitress appeared with a tray of glasses, a jug of beer and bowls of peanuts. Poppy, not normally a beer-drinker, accepted a glass of the icy-cold amber fluid. As it trickled down her throat she was surprised at how good it tasted, and put it down to the heat.

Jen raised her glass. 'Welcome.'

'Thanks. It's been an interesting start.' And the perfect segue into the information she wanted. 'I'm sorry if I got you into trouble with Matt on Sunday.'

'No worries. Matt has good days and bad, and they're hard to pick so we just roll with them.' Jen fiddled with a thick cardboard coaster already damp from condensation. 'It's been an awful eighteen months. It's hard to know what to do or say when someone goes through something like that, you know?'

Something like what? Cancer? Car accident? 'How did—?'

'Hi, sorry I'm late!' Sarah Fielding, Poppy's theatre nurse, slid into the bench seat, all sparkling green eyes, wild red hair and a handbag the size of the Outback. She looked very different from the competent woman who'd made the morning's theatre session run so smoothly. 'Justin got home earlier than I thought and as the kids were already in bed we took advantage of it.' She winked and raised a glass. 'To fast sex.'

Jen laughed and clinked glasses with Sarah and threw Poppy a conspiratorial grin. 'To long-distance phone sex. David's out in the Kimberley for another month.'

The hairs on Poppy's arms stood up. God, this was why she never went out in a group. Joking about sex with women she barely knew wasn't something she was comfortable doing.

Let's face it, you're not comfortable doing sex, full stop.

Shut up.

But she wasn't fast enough and the memory of Steven's voice echoed through her. *Sexually, a fridge is warmer.*

She realised with a jolt that the two women were staring at her, expecting a response to the toast. She gripped the edge of the table to keep her hand from touching her pendant. 'Actually, I'm not planning on having sex here.'

Jen's eyes blazed with interest. 'So it's phone sex for you, too. Have you left a gorgeous man behind in Perth, pining for you?'

'Uh, no.' *He left me.*

Jen's brows rose in surprise. 'So you're unattached?'

Poppy sipped her beer against a tight throat, wishing she could mutter a magic word and conveniently vanish. She didn't do this sort of chitchat well, and she was even worse when the focus was on her. 'I am, and I came here to work. Given the amount there is to do, I won't have time for sex.'

'You can't go three months without sex!' Sarah's expression combined abject horror with good-natured scheming and she glanced around the bar as if she was looking for someone.

'Oh, I can *easily* go three months.' Poppy drained her glass.

But it was as if Sarah hadn't heard her and she turned back, her face fill of dismay. 'Damien isn't here tonight but, Poppy, you have to meet him. He's the new flying doctor pilot. He's totally gorgeous, unattached and he'd be the perfect diversion for you.'

She was having trouble trying to align this sex-obsessed woman with the one who'd been so professional this morning, and it took a lot of effort to keep the biting tone out of her voice. 'I don't need diverting.'

'We all need diverting. Life in this town is tough.' Sarah gave a sincere and friendly smile with no agenda, while she refilled Poppy's glass.

Poppy stuck to her mantra. 'I came here to do a job, pure and simple.'

'But why not have some fun at the same time?' Sarah tucked her curls behind her ear. 'Damien would be the perfect reward for being stuck out here, although you will have a bit of healthy competition from every other single woman in town and probably the occasional married one as well. Any single, professional man who arrives is immediately considered as a ticket out of here, or a way of making the town work for you.'

Poppy smiled stiffly. 'Well, I don't need a ticket out because I've got a huge job back in Perth.'

Not necessarily. She tried to close her mind to the undermining thought and at the same time wrestle back some control in the conversation. She spun the spotlight back on Sarah and raised her brows. 'So, did marrying Justin make this town work for you?'

Sarah laughed; a big, congenial chuckle. 'Touché, Poppy. OK, I get it—you don't want to be matched up. But to answer your question, Justin and I met in Canberra during his intern year. He came out here as a med student, fell in love with the Outback and wanted to come back. As I loved him, I said I'd come out for a couple of years and see if I could love it too.'

Love *and* career support. The answer slugged Poppy, totally demolishing her preconceived ideas and stabbing her with a combination of jealousy and remorse. Sarah had what she'd never been able to achieve. 'And?'

Sarah shrugged. 'It's a man's town and there needs to be more of a focus on the women. I'm on the neighbourhood house committee and we're setting up groups based on interests that we hope will spin off into support, mentoring and friendship groups.' Her face suddenly lit up. 'Hey, what else are you good at besides surgery?'

She tried to focus on the unexpected question. 'What do you mean?'

'Hobbies, interests, things like that.'

Her mind was a blank space because for years all she'd done was haul herself up the surgical ladder with long and punishing hours, leaving no time for anything other than sleep. Often there'd been scant time for that. 'The last few years have all been about work.'

'What's on your "to-do" list? What do you crave to do when you have the time?' Jen leaned forward, her eyes filled with unexpected sympathy.

Poppy bristled at the look. Why on earth would a nurse be feeling sorry for her? But her usually quick and logical mind struggled to think of an answer to the question. Desperate to banish Jen's air of pity, she dug deep but nothing surfaced. 'I've always wanted to...' God, what had she always wanted to do?

Win.

Win Dad's love. Steven's love.

She grasped at straws, needing to give them something, needing to show them she was a successful woman in control of her life *and* with interests. Interests she didn't have. For some reason, she thought of how she enjoyed singing in the shower and belting out a tune. Shower singing was something she did most mornings and it reminded her of how she'd sung in the choir at school and at uni. Singing would do as an answer. 'I'd go back to music and rejoin a choir.'

Sarah squealed and clapped her hands together. 'You sing? That's fantastic.' She high-fived Jen.

Another prickle of apprehension washed through Poppy, this time stronger than the last. 'Have I missed something?'

Sarah beamed. 'I've wanted to start a women's choir because it's so much more than just singing and so many women here would benefit. Jen plays piano and now you've arrived with choral experience so we have a musical director. It's just perfect!'

'Musical director?' She heard her voice rise and she shook her head hard. 'I don't have time for something like that.'

Sarah's eyes narrowed and her carefree aura vanished, replaced with a very professional and determined one. 'Poppy, you're a successful woman in a field dominated by men and that makes you a mentor. We have women here who are isolated, living in tough conditions, dealing with their partners' shiftwork and dislocated from their families because they've followed their partners out here for work. It can all add up to depression and low self-esteem.' The passion in her voice carried clearly out above the noise of the room. She leaned forward. 'I know you're busy but seeing as you're so adamant about not having sex while you're here...' she winked '...that frees up time for some community service. Think of it as improving women's health, and as a doctor you can hardly walk away from that.'

Checkmate.

Poppy wanted to plead too much work and no time

but she knew both these women were intimate with her workload and would juggle rosters to create the time for her if she didn't find it herself. Sarah, with her air of good fun and no cares, had her over a barrel with her well-developed sense of social justice.

Poppy sighed. 'We start small, right?'

Sarah gave a long, slow smile. 'We'll start with who-ever's interested.'

Poppy reluctantly raised her glass. 'To the Bundallagong's women's choir.'

'To the choir and friendship.' Jen titled her glass to-wards Poppy's and gave her a wide, open smile.

'To fun, friendship and service.' Sarah joined the toast.

A flurry of movement caught Poppy's eye and she turned towards the door. A tall man had entered and was crossing the room towards the bar, where he pulled up a stool and sat down next to another man. The chatter of the room dropped for a moment as all the women turned and followed his movements.

She instantly recognised Matt as the guy already sit-ting, his wild hair gleaming like a dark and rumpled halo in complete contrast to the golden fire of the man next to him. Side by side the two men looked like light and dark, storm and sunshine. Her gaze should have been tempted by the freshness, youth and sheer vitality of the unknown man but instead it was stalled on Matt. Stalled on the way his hair curled around his ears, stalled on his toned shoulders that filled out his shirt, giving it a precise and square fit; stalled on him full-stop.

'The blond delight is Damien and you have the right to change your mind about sex but not the choir.' Sarah leaned back with a conspiratorial smile on her lips. 'Rumour has it he can take a woman flying in more ways than one.'

Matt had been quietly getting drunk when Damien had arrived. He hoped that after one drink, the pilot would be taken away by one, two or more of the many women who'd been waiting so patiently for his arrival. That would mean he could resume his relationship with the barman, and wipe himself out for the night.

It had been a very long time since he'd got drunk, but during the first few weeks after returning to Bundallagong, alone, it had been a regular event. It had been the only surefire way to stop the dreams that broke his sleep and took him back to the heart of his grief, never allowing him any time to breathe without it. But the morning he'd woken up on the back steps after sleeping rough because he hadn't been able to work out how to put the key in the lock had been the day he'd stopped drinking hard. That, and the fact he knew it was a very fine line between himself and the alcoholics he treated in Emergency.

He'd been sober for weeks. He'd even started running again at dawn now he was able to get out of bed without a thundering headache, but Poppy Stanfield's arrival had changed everything. The only way he was going home tonight was completely buzzed so he could fall into the black oblivion of deep and uninterrupted sleep.

He threw back a shot. God, he hated himself. He despised the way he couldn't get Poppy out of his mind when he should be honouring Lisa's memory. He couldn't believe that on Monday night he'd left the hospital on time and cooked a meal in anticipation of

Poppy's arrival home. All day she'd jumped in and out of his thoughts and he'd found himself looking forward to sitting down at a table with her, hearing about her day and sharing his own with a living person rather than the silent walls of the house.

But he'd eaten alone. By 10:00 p.m. he'd thrown out the food and gone to bed—to bed but not to sleep. His silent monologue had veered between cursing life in general that he no longer had Lisa and Annie, and cursing himself that he'd been so pathetic as to think he could try and have a normal evening, although he had no clue what normal was any more. He'd heard her car pull in at midnight and when he'd finally fallen asleep, his dreams had been filled with a woman who had looked like Lisa but whenever he'd got close, he could only see vibrant blue eyes. Poppy's eyes.

He spoke to the barman. 'I'll have another Scotch and...' He turned to the pilot. 'What can I buy you, Damien?'

'Soda water, thanks, I'm on call. Your night off?'

'Yep.'

'Hey, Doc, third drink in an hour—time for your keys.' Lewis, the barman, held out a container with a couple of sets of car keys at the bottom.

'I walked, Lew.' He had a standing arrangement with the barman so he avoided doing anything really stupid. A couple of times soon after Lisa's death, when being alive had almost been too much to bear, he'd got way too close to stupid.

'Good to hear it.' Lewis slid the two drinks across the counter.

Damien sipped his and surveyed the room. 'So how's that guy I flew down to Perth the other night getting on?'

'Not bad. You'll probably be transporting him back here in a couple of weeks.'

Damien raised his hand in a wave and Matt glanced around to see who'd caught his attention. With a shot of surprise he recognised Sarah Fielding. Why on earth was Sarah beckoning Damien?

She and Lisa had been firm friends from the moment the Fieldings had arrived in town and as a result the two young families had socialised together a lot. Since coming back to Bundallagong, he'd only seen Justin at hospital functions and at the GP in-service he conducted every few months. He hadn't been able to face a social gathering with Sarah and the kids.

He stared at her and then made out Jen's profile behind her, before realising there was a third person at the table.

Surprise rolled through him. Poppy sat on a chair, looking awkward and completely out of place.

Sarah arrived at the bar, her gaze cautious, and she seemed to breathe in before she spoke. 'Justin was sorry you didn't make golf the other day, Matt. He's on for next Wednesday and looking for a partner, so call him?'

He didn't want to play golf. 'Sure.'

She nodded, her expression worried, and then she turned and gave Damien a flirty smile. Sliding her arm through the pilot's, she urged, 'Come and meet our new surgeon. She has the most amazing eyes you've ever seen and is in town for three months with no one to play with.'

Damien looked over Sarah's head towards the table of women. 'Ebony and ivory?'

Matt didn't like the way the pilot was scoping out Poppy and his voice came out on a growl. 'That's her, but be warned: just like a praying mantis, she'll play with you and then she'll eat you.'

But instead of being put off, the pilot grinned. 'I love a challenge.' He slid off the bar stool and strode towards the table.

The thought of Damien hitting on Poppy had Matt up and off the stool. *What are you doing? She'll probably tear strips off glamour boy and even if she doesn't, what do you care?*

But he picked his drink up anyway and let his feet carry him to the table. He arrived just as Damien was suggesting to Poppy that the only way to really appreciate the Pilbara was from the air.

Poppy's fine black brows rose in a look Matt was starting to recognise as pure sarcasm. 'If flying means not missing out on every single millimetre of the thousands of kilometres of endless, flat gibber plain and red dust, yes, I suspect you're right. Fortunately I flew in on a clear day so I don't feel the need repeat it any time soon.'

Damien looked slightly taken aback that his usual invitation had failed and Matt hid a smile before sitting down next to Poppy. Her fresh floral scent hinted at the newness of spring and it spun around him, urging every cell in his body to lean in close and breathe deeply. 'Actually, the only way to appreciate the unconventional beauty of this area is by four-wheel drive and getting a hands-on perspective.'

'Unconventional is right.' Poppy's fingers closed around the base of the pendant at her neck.

Jen's quizzical expression moved between Poppy and Matt. 'Matt's right. You should make sure you visit Walker's Gorge while you're here.'

'It's a fair distance from here, though. I could fly you in,' Damien countered. 'Just let me know when you have a free day.'

Poppy's hand fell back to her lap and she gave a short laugh. 'That's very kind but given that my surgical list is endless, and Sarah's already shanghaied me into starting a women's choir, I think my time in Bundallagong is pretty much full.'

A choir. Matt did a double-take, not able to imagine her in a musical role, but was that just another piece of the puzzle that was Poppy? His eyes met hers and he watched the vivid blue of her irises almost disappear into rapidly dilating inky discs. A flash of undisguised attraction burned bright for a heartbeat and then faded, but not before a wave of her heat crashed into him. Like a chain reaction, every part of him vibrated with hungry need.

She pulled her gaze away and rose to her feet, her movements jerky. 'Thanks, everyone, for the welcome drinks. It was really kind but it's time to call it a night.'

Damien moved towards her. *No way, mate.* For the second time, Matt found himself shooting to his feet and he spoke without thinking. 'I'll come with you.'

Her fingers tugged at the fine, silver pendant and her expression mixed hesitation with determination. 'Really, there's no need.'

But he wasn't letting her leave alone or giving

glamour boy an opening so he shrugged casually. 'I need the ride.' Instinctively, he slid his hand into the small of her back and guided her around the group, through the crowd and out into the night, ignoring the stunned looks of his colleagues.

The heat from Matt's hand flooded Poppy, streaming through her veins like hot vapour and culminating in a tingling pond of undeniable lust. Her breath came too fast and the muscles in her legs threatened to melt as the sensations spun through her with their intoxicating promise of pleasure.

Pull yourself together. It's just the touch of a well-mannered man. Steven had exemplary manners and remember what happened? The thought grounded her momentarily. Gathering her tattered self-control, she passed through the doorway into the starlit night and stepped away from his touch.

She hadn't been surprised that Matt had been drinking alone at the bar, given the way he held himself aloof from people and coupled with the townsfolk not seeming to know how to treat him, but the fact he'd joined them at the table had caught her off guard. His offer to leave with her had totally floored her. From the moment he'd sat down next to her she'd struggled to keep up with the conversation as every part of her had been absorbed by his closeness.

Now his gaze stayed fixed on her, and she shivered. *Find your strength, defuse the tension.* 'Where's your car?'

'At home.' He had no trouble matching her stride. Unlike her stiff and jerky gait, his was fluid. 'I walked because I'd planned to drink more than the legal driving limit.'

He didn't look drunk and she wouldn't call him relaxed but something about him was different. Less guarded perhaps? 'And have you?'

'Probably.' He leaned casually against the car, waiting, with his toned arms crossed over his T-shirt-clad chest and the light from the streetlamp spilling over him. It gave him the quintessential look of a bad boy.

Her mouth dried and her well of strength drained away. Flustered, she dropped her gaze and fumbled in her handbag, searching for her car keys. She breathed out in relief when her fingers closed over metal and she quickly activated the lock release button and swung up into the vehicle. She just had to get through a short drive. How hard could that be?

He sat down next to her, filling the cabin with his fresh scent of laundry soap and everything male. She let it fill her nostrils, pour into her lungs, and suddenly her hands trembled.

Intelligent brown eyes zeroed in. 'You OK to drive? We could always walk.'

'I'm fine.' *Liar.* She wasn't drunk but she was a long way from fine. With Matt so close her brain had closed down under the assault of her body's wayward pleasure-seeking mission and she couldn't think straight. She hit the on button of the radio with the palm of her hand, filling the cabin with music, and then she planted her foot. She tried valiantly to focus on the music but even that was against her with a raunchy song about make-up sex. Her hand wanted to leave the steering wheel, reach out and press her palm against the stubble on his cheek. She turned left at the first intersection and right at the second, and then drove straight.

'Uh, Poppy?'

'What?' It came out far too snappy as her body mocked her every good intention to stay aloof by sending rafts of hot and cold streaking though her.

He tilted his head, a lock of hair falling forward. 'I'm not so drunk that I don't notice where we are. You're going the wrong direction and the house is back that way.'

She squinted through the windshield. Oh, God, he was right. With her mind complete mush, she'd taken the wrong turning at the first intersection and now she had no clue where she was. 'It all looks the same at night.'

'Sure, it pretty much does except for the bright lights of the port, which gives you a whopping big navigational tool.' His voiced teased as he turned towards her, his face clear in the moonlight. His mouth was curved up into a broad smile, a smile that banished the usual hovering sadness as it raced to his eyes, creasing the edges and making them dazzle with fun and wicked intent.

She almost drove off the road.

She'd wondered what he'd look like when he truly smiled and now she knew—completely devastating. Hauling her gaze back to the road and loathing herself on so many levels for her total lack of control over her body, she tried desperately not to sneak another look at his sexy grin. Usually when she was proved wrong she got defensive, but there was something about the unexpected softness that had momentarily surrounded him that made her laugh. 'I'll concede you have a point.' She slowed in preparation to do a U-turn.

'Keep going. We're pretty close to Estuary Road and you get a great view of the town from there. It looks pretty at night.'

She changed gears. 'What, no red dust?'

'The key to Bundallagong is to focus on the ocean. The turtles and the whales will amaze you.' He stretched out his arm. 'Turn here.'

The headlights beamed onto a break in the trees and she slowly navigated the vehicle down a narrow track. 'Are you sure this is a road?'

He leaned back in his seat. 'You're such a city girl. Live a little.'

'I live plenty.' *You love deluding yourself, don't you?*

The track opened up into a wide parking area with a boat ramp and she parked. Matt jumped out of the car and quickly walked round the front of the vehicle, reaching her door before she'd finished unlatching her seat belt. Surprise piggybacked on every other rampaging emotion.

He opened her door. 'Come on, you need to see this.'

She followed him across the stony area until they stood on the curve of the bay. Across the moonlit water, the massive port with its heavy equipment that looked like a scar on the landscape during the day sparkled white, yellow, blue and orange. 'I concede it has its own charm.'

He laughed—a rich, deep sound that made her think of the bass notes of a clarinet. 'Careful, Poppy, you're in danger of gushing.'

He stood so close to her she could feel his heat, hear his breathing and smell his spicy scent—all of it swirling around her, taunting her to reach out and grab it for herself. 'It's nothing like I expected.'

His head leaned in, his eyes smoky and intense. 'Nothing ever is.'

'No.' She barely got the word out as his breath

caressed her face and her heart bruised itself against her ribs. She spoke almost as much to ground herself as to reply. 'I belong in Perth.'

'Who really belongs anywhere?' His warm hand slid along her jaw, and then long, strong fingers tilted her head. His dark hair fell forward, stroking her cheek, before his lips brushed hers—soft, hot, partially testing but mostly firm and sure.

He tasted of malt, tropical heat and arousal. He was kissing her and, God help her, she wanted it like her body needed air. Her hand wrapped around the back of his head and she pulled him into her, feeling the hard muscles of his thighs pressing against her and his heart thundering against her own. He murmured a groan and his tongue flicked at her closed lips, seeking entry, and she opened them to him, needing to have him inside her, wanting him to explore, lick, taste and take. Wanting him to treat her like a woman.

Every part of her burned as Matt's expert mouth dismantled any lingering doubts that kissing him was a bad idea. She kissed him back. She kissed away the past, banishing Steven's cold, hard voice and releasing the barrier on her femininity, letting it flood her and then flood Matt.

He gasped, his hands tangling in her hair and then gripping her head to gain access to her throat. He trailed spine-tingling kisses along her jaw before dropping his head lower, tracing the hollow of her neck with his tongue. She sagged against him as she heard a mewling sound in the back of her throat.

She hauled his mouth back to her own, needing that intimate contact and tasting salt and her own heady desire. Nothing mattered except losing herself in the heat of that hot, throbbing place, and she turned herself over to its power, allowing her mind to spin out on bliss and her body to burn.

She was boneless, wet with need, weak with longing yet strong with the power of her body and she gloried in it. His hand covered her breast, the thin material of her blouse and bra feeling like a concrete slab between them. She wanted to feel the heat of his palm against her skin, let the weight of her breast fill his hand, and she ached for the graze of his thumb on her tightening nipple. She popped her shirt open and guided his hand. 'Touch me.'

His body stiffened against hers, rigid from head to toe, and suddenly his hands were on her shoulders, pushing. He ripped his mouth from hers, stepping back, breaking the kiss, breaking all contact.

'This is a mistake.' His words shredded the night air—harsh, ragged and uncompromising.

You're a machine, Poppy, not a woman. The memory of Steven's voice taunted and the fire in her body chilled to ice. Her legs shook, followed by the rest of her, and she desperately wanted to evaporate like water against parched ground. Instead, she lifted her chin, locked down every emotion and pulled her blouse shut tight. 'That's what they all say.'

She strode to the car, slamming the door against his voice, and gunned the vehicle out of the car park, not caring how the hell he got home.

CHAPTER FIVE

'EXACTLY *where* is Victor Chu's fluid balance chart?' Matt's head pounded and the backs of his eyes ached.

Jen frowned but her mouth moved into an anxious smile. 'It's clipped to his chart board.'

'If it was there, I wouldn't be asking.' He spun the chart board so it skidded across the desk. 'His pulmonary oedema is worsening and he's now on a strict fluid intake, which I'd write on the chart, if I could find it.'

She pulled the sheaf of charts out of the folder and started going through them one by one. 'You don't look very well. Do you need some of my winning combination of complex B and C vitamin drink?'

'I'm *not* hungover.'

She smiled overly brightly as if she didn't believe him and produced the elusive, pink, fluid balance chart.

'I'm not.' He sighed and tried to swallow his defensive tone. 'I had a terrible night and no sleep.' He wrote his orders on the chart and added a new drug regime in an attempt to dry Victor's lungs and maximise the effectiveness of the weak beats of an old and tired heart. 'I just need coffee.'

'There's a fresh pot in the lounge.'

He nodded his thanks and backed away from her

sympathetic glance. He didn't deserve it. Not this time when his lack of sleep had nothing to do with grief and everything to do with Poppy. God, why on earth had he kissed her?

But he knew why. He'd had plenty of time to think about it as he'd walked the three kilometres home. He poured himself a large mug of the aromatic brew and closed his eyes, instantly seeing Poppy's plump, lush lips. He forced his lids open but it didn't help—he could still see the after-image of their shape and colour, and that, combined with those startling eyes, had him almost permanently hard. It had rendered his restraint so thin it was friable. Last night, standing so close to her under that bright, white moon, with her intoxicating perfume spinning around him and her body heat rolling into his, it had all combined to demolish the tattered shreds of his self-control. All he'd known was that he'd ached to touch her, craved to taste her, and hungered to savour her.

So he had.

And she'd flooded him with unforeseen and unre-strained passion. Passion that had roared through him, feeding his desire with so much fuel that he'd almost combusted on the spot. His body had taken over, empty-ing his mind of everything except the white-hot pleasure of sex. And he'd revelled in it. It had been so long since he'd felt alive like that and nothing had existed except two hot bodies seeking each other.

Touch me. Her tremulous and breathy voice had sliced through him, penetrating his lust-fogged mind like a knife and dumping reality upon him as he'd real-ised who he'd been kissing.

Not Lisa. Hell, he'd had his tongue down the throat of

another woman and it hadn't been enough: he'd wanted so much more.

So he'd pulled away, despising himself for betraying Lisa.

What about betraying Poppy?

He stifled a groan and slugged more coffee. He hadn't seen her since she'd stormed away from him and he'd been in no state then to even try and call her back. Even if his mind and voice had worked, he knew she would never have stopped to listen and he'd been incapable of telling her the truth.

'Matt, ambulance is pulling in,' Jen called out as she hurried towards the ambulance bay.

Matt joined her, glad to be distracted from the mess he'd created, and he pulled on gloves, ready to treat the young man writhing in pain on the ambulance's stretcher. 'What happened?'

'His apprentice said he'd been lifting concrete slabs and went down screaming. I gave him some nitrous but he's still in pain.' Doug Finlay, the senior paramedic, gave a brief handover.

'Hernia?' Jen muttered, before moving to transfer the man onto the trolley, but as she reached his side she paused in surprise. 'Liam?'

Matt instantly recognised one of the town's builders and based on what the ambulance officer had said thought an abdominal or spinal disc hernia were very possible. 'Where does it hurt? Your back?'

Liam shook his head, his expression a combination of pain and embarrassment. 'It's *not* my back.'

Matt caught the look. 'Ah, Jen, can you go and start the paperwork.'

'Sure.'

As the door closed behind her, Liam started to dry-retch and Matt grabbed a kidney dish. 'As soon as I've examined you, I can give you something for the pain.'

'I remember being kicked in the balls when I was aa kid but this—' He seemed to have trouble breathing against the pain. 'This is absolute agony.'

Matt nodded sympathetically. 'I want to rule out a couple of other possibilities.' He palpated Liam's abdomen and groin but he couldn't feel a hernia. 'I need to examine your testicles.'

Liam barely nodded as his white-knuckled hands gripped the silver railing of the trolley.

'I think you've got a torsion of the testicle.'

Liam looked blank. 'What?'

'It's twisted.' He pulled the ultrasound over and examined the area. He pointed to the screen. 'There's the problem.'

Liam looked like he could hardly focus. 'It's absolute agony.'

'That's because the blood supply is being restricted.' He saved the picture, wiped the Doppler and returned it to its holder.

A knock sounded on the door and Matt tossed the modesty sheet over Liam as he called, 'Come in.'

Jen entered the room, followed by a woman who appeared to be a similar age to his patient. She rushed towards Liam, picking up his hand. 'I came as soon as Tim called me.'

Jen slung the clipboard over the end of the trolley and said quietly to Matt, 'Should I page Poppy?'

Matt tilted his head in agreement.

Jen returned it as she spoke. 'This is Emma Waterson—Liam's fiancée.'

Emma, still holding Liam's hand, looked up, her forehead creased with worry. 'What's wrong with him?'

Matt filled her in on his diagnosis and watched her face pale.

'Why...? I mean, how did it happen?'

'It's not an uncommon condition in men under twenty-five and I'd say Liam probably has a genetic or structural weakness. Combine that with heavy lifting, and it would be enough to cause the twist.'

She turned accusingly to her fiancé. 'You told me you were getting the bobcat in to lift that concrete.'

Liam blanched as another wave of pain hit him. 'Em, I'm sorry. I couldn't get it today and I was trying to get everything done so we could have a two-week honeymoon.'

Emma let out a wail. 'Oh, God, the wedding. Can you untwist it?'

Matt tried to suppress a shudder. 'Liam needs surgery. The good news is that we have a surgeon here.' *Good news for Liam, anyway.*

'Good news?' The soon-to-be bride swayed on her feet. 'That means there's bad news too. Will it mean we can't have children?'

'If the testicle has to be removed, the other one won't be affected.'

'And the honeymoon?' Liam grimaced as he moved.

Matt gave a wry smile. The guy was in agony but still thinking about sex. *It's all you've been thinking about today.*

He rubbed his temple. 'You'll be a bit tender for a day or so but the second week you should be just fine.'

Liam sunk back on the pillows. 'In that case, do your worst—just stop the pain.'

'I can do that.' Poppy strode into the room, her blue eyes flashing brightly.

With her green theatre scrubs floating around her and concealing the soft curves Matt knew nestled underneath, she gave him an almost imperceptible nod before studying the ultrasound screen.

Liam choked. 'You're the surgeon?'

Poppy gave a restrained smile. 'I understand you'd probably feel more comfortable with a man but think of it as taking one for all the women in the world who find themselves being treated by male gynaecologists.'

Emma laughed. 'I like her.'

'You're not the one going under the knife,' Liam grumbled.

'Poor baby, I'm sure she'll be gentle.'

Matt didn't disillusion either of them with his thoughts.

After Poppy had explained the procedure and obtained consent, he followed her out of the room, thankful they had a patient to discuss. 'I'll put in an IV, take some blood for FBC, U&Es and cross-matching, and then he's all yours.'

She raised her well-shaped jet brows. 'As long as you're sure. I'd hate it if you made a mistake.' Hurt shimmered around the sarcasm.

He swallowed a groan. It was time to make some sort of restitution. 'I wanted to talk to you this morning but you left before dawn.'

She folded her arms, scrunching the scrubs tightly over her breasts. 'Ah, the apology. No need, heard it before.'

Apology? What apology? But his gaze snagged on the outline of her bra and he swallowed, hard, forcing his mind to stay on track with the conversation. 'How can you have heard it before? I haven't ever apologised to you.'

She rolled her eyes, azure deepening to midnight. 'You're a man, I'm a woman. Believe me, I've heard it and I've heard every single excuse in the book of sorry. I don't have time for this, Matt. I'm due in surgery.'

He trapped his angry retort and watched her walk away. *Believe me, I've heard it.* What the hell did that mean? Did she think she could throw off some line and just keep walking?

Well, what did you really expect? He had no clue. Damn it, he hadn't actually planned on apologising. She'd been an equal participant in the kiss and this was 2011. Surely people had a right to change their minds.

You touched her breast; it had gone way past a kiss.

He tried to recall the sequence of events last night after his head had roared so loudly with the realisation of what he'd been doing—when betrayal and lust had collided and he'd pulled back.

This is a mistake.

That's what they all say.

Who the hell were 'they'?

This time Matt didn't cook. He didn't go to bed at 10:00 p.m. Or eleven. He opened the door to Poppy at eleven-fifteen.

Shocked surprise crossed her face and she quickly glanced towards her house before staring straight back at him. 'Two houses, both have rats.'

Anger scorched his intention to invite her to sit down and calmly talk this mess out. 'Oh, and that's really mature.' He ran his hand through his hair, trying to find the calm he'd once been known for. 'Look, we have to work together and right now we're sharing a house, so what do you need me to say so we can go back to being semi-civil with each other?'

'Nothing.' She tried to move past him.

He blocked her. 'That's rubbish. If it was nothing you wouldn't have left me out at the point last night to walk home.'

She shrugged. 'You told me you were planning on walking home anyway.'

'From the pub!' He heard his voice rise. 'Which is three minutes away, not three kilometres.'

Her stony expression wavered slightly with the tiniest mark of contrition, and he pounced on it as a sign of a chance at reconciliation. 'Do you want a drink?'

Her brows rose. 'Isn't that what got you into trouble last night?'

'I was *not* drunk.' For the second time that day, he ground out the indignant words. 'Six months ago you could have levelled that accusation at me but not last night.'

The faintest tremble wove across her bottom lip before she snagged it with her teeth. Teeth that had nipped at his lips last night in the frenzy of *that* kiss. The memory sent a bolt of heat through him and he realised he was staring at her mouth.

Her chin shot up. 'So you were sober. That makes it worse. I have to say, this is one hell of an apology.'

'I'm not apologising.' The yelled words shot around them both, loud and uncompromising.

She blinked and then spoke quietly. 'No, you're not.'

She walked past him, leaving him standing in the hall, stunned.

Your manners always made me feel special.

Lisa's voice chided him. He'd never yelled at a woman in his life so what the hell was wrong with him? He leaned against the wall and slowed his breathing before walking into the kitchen. Poppy had poured herself a glass of sauvignon blanc from the bottle he'd put in the fridge earlier, and was staring out into the night.

'I'm sorry, I shouldn't have yelled. I don't usually yell.'

She didn't turn round but her shoulders stiffened so much that balls could have bounced off them. 'Yeah, well, I've been known to have that effect on men. That and not being woman enough. Congratulations. You've gone two for two and you're up there with the best.'

He felt like the floor was tilting under his feet and he was left scrabbling for purchase while careering inexorably into a black sinkhole. 'What are you talking about?'

She spun to face him, her face pinched as conflicting emotions broke through her usually impenetrable armour. 'You want me to spell it out to you?' Her voice rose and she dragged in a breath. 'I'm an exceptional surgeon but a lousy kisser. I'm sorry it was such a disappointment for you.'

Her words hit with the velocity of a missile, stunning him. 'That's what you think?' He picked up his bottle of water, trying to assemble coherent thought. 'You think you're bad at kissing? Why on earth would you think that?'

A shudder whipped across her shoulders, round her

torso and down her long, long legs. 'Oh, let me see. It started at high school with my name scrawled all over the boys' toilets, then my ex-husband mentioned it as often as he could and, hmm, last night you told me it was a mistake.'

That's what they all say. Her words from last night lanced him and then all-encompassing anger at an un-known man erupted so fast it turned his breath fiery. 'Your ex-husband doesn't know squat.'

Her pupils dilated, drowning her shimmering cornflower-blue irises, and she swallowed, the ripple of movement centred in the hollow of her throat. The place he'd branded last night. The plastic bottle of water crunched loudly under his tightening fingers.

She shrugged. 'Yeah, well, let's not go there.'

'Poppy, believe me, you can kiss.' The husky words somehow passed through his tight throat and he downed some water, trying to douse his burning need for her.

She bit her lip as her hand crawled to her pendant. 'Don't do this, Matt. I'm not a child and you can't muddy the truth. It stands and it has done for a long time. It stood loud and clear last night out at the point. For whatever reason, you were moved to kiss me. I kissed you back and you pulled away. End of story. We'll both live.'

Despite everything, he knew their kiss had fired life into parts of his body that had been numb for a long time. Poppy had done that with her mouth, her tongue, her teeth and her taste. He couldn't let her continue to believe she was a lousy kisser. *So tell her why you pulled back.*

But he couldn't do it. He didn't want to have *that*

conversation, and see and hear her pity. With a growl he forced out, 'You've obviously been kissing the wrong men.'

She gave a derisive laugh, her face tight with the pain of her past. 'Yeah, well, last night was a case in point.'

No, it wasn't. In two strides he stood next to her, cupping her cheeks and pressing his mouth softly to hers. Taking a gamble to prove a point, a point she needed to understand.

She stiffened, her lips closed to him. Gently, his tongue ventured along the outline of those wondrous bee-stung lips, lips that drove him crazy on an hourly basis, and he tasted a hint of gooseberry and restraint born of hurt. But she didn't push him away so he slowly nibbled her generous bottom lip, coaxing it to open and unlock the ambrosia he knew waited within.

He heard a strangled moan and recognised the moment her inherent sexuality defeated her control. Her mouth—hot, moist and seeking—met his with a scorch of fire, lighting a blaze that tore though him, revisiting places and invading untouched parts of him. He buried his hands in her hair and her fingers dug into his scalp, as if it was the only way she could stay standing.

His skin, slick with sweat, tingled with something he barely recognised because the memory of it had faded to fuzzy faintness—hedonistic pleasure. He lost himself, amazed at how decadent yet occasionally sweet and tender her mouth could be. His tongue met hers in a dance of wonder that ignited into a fevered duel, each of them angling for control and driven crazy by need.

The power surge of her desire lit up the back of his mind.

When did you ever kiss Lisa like this in this house?

The thought shocked him so hard his mouth slackened and he almost fell.

Poppy's eyes, glazed with ecstasy's bliss, instantly focused. She pulled away, her breasts rising and falling with fast, shallow breaths. 'What the hell is happening? You're doing it again.'

This time, with the light of the room, he glimpsed raw and pulsating pain in the electric blue of her eyes before her steely control shut it down.

He closed his eyes against his own pain, shame, guilt and utter despair. *She doesn't deserve this.* Forcing himself to look at her, he knew with gut-wrenching certainty what had to come next. 'It's not you, Poppy, it's me.'

Poppy stared at him, barely able to catch her breath and hardly able to believe her ears. Her heart pumped desire-fuelled blood through her, making her skittish and demolishing her usually logical thought processes. It took more than effort to clear her head. She scraped her mussed hair out of her eyes and clamped it by tightening the now loose band, the action giving her precious moments to pull herself together. 'I don't understand.'

His hand ploughed through his hair as his expression became imploring. 'Please believe me when I tell you that you're not *just* an exceptional surgeon.'

A kernel of belief almost sprouted inside her, but words counted little against crystal clear actions. He'd pulled away from her twice and both times had ended the most bone-melting kisses she'd even known. He'd rejected her, like all the men in her life. 'I get the feeling there's a "but" coming.'

His eyelids hooded his dark eyes, masking his emotions, but his body betrayed him when his left hand fisted so tightly his knuckles gleamed white. When he finally spoke it sounded like it was coming from the depths of his soul. 'You're the first woman I've kissed since Lisa died.'

Poppy's legs gave way and she sat down hard on the couch. Oh, dear God, how had she been so dumb? She wanted to bury her face in her hands at her thoughtless and completely selfish neediness. Last night, when he'd stopped kissing her, her past had come rushing back so hard and fast it had obliterated any other possible reasons as to why he'd stepped back. By default, she'd made it all about herself, when in reality it was about him.

She had no idea what to say except the obvious. 'You loved her very much.'

'I do.'

And right then, with the blinding clarity of the hind-sight, she understood. 'Kissing me is like cheating on Lisa.'

He sat down on the opposite end of the couch, his expression tinged with apologetic regret. 'Yeah.'

She wondered what it would be like to be loved by someone so much that they considered it an act of faith-lessness to kiss someone else even when you were dead. Steven hadn't loved her enough in life to be faithful and yet she wasn't certain she'd want a lover to be racked with this much guilt after she'd gone. Had she done something to trigger memories? 'Do I remind you of her?'

'God, no!'

She took the hit, feeling it reverberate through her with a dull ache, which was dumb because of course he loved his wife.

Show no hurt. She tilted her head in irony. 'Just as long as you're sure.'

He had the grace to look abashed. 'Sorry.'

'Don't be.' She grabbed her wine and took a gulp, trying to dig down to find the mature adult. His emphatic reply spoke volumes: she was nothing like his wife and no matter how that made her feel it gave her the opening to ask the question that had been on the tip of her tongue from the moment she'd discovered he was a widower. 'So what was Lisa like?'

Her name. Matt stared at Poppy for a moment, realising that no one in town ever said Lisa's name to him any more. He turned away, doggedly looking out through the patio doors, uncomfortable about the comparison he was about to make. 'She was blonde to your black and short to your tall.' *Her mouth wasn't as full as yours.* He banished the thought by trying to focus on Lisa but his mental image of her face clouded around the edges. 'She had a way with people, an ability to find something uniquely special about them. It made you feel like you were the only person who mattered to her at that moment in time. She made friends easily but she also kept them. There was something about her that made you want to try and be the best person you could.'

'She sounds...exceptional.' Poppy's voice was strained and she cleared her throat.

'She was.' He kept staring out into the night as memories sucked at him, threatening to drown him, and he fought not to go to that dark place.

Poppy placed her glass on the side table and the noise of glass on wood brought him back to the present. She rose to her feet, the movement fluid yet extremely controlled, right down to the way the last hair on her head settled into place. He remembered the first time he'd met her and thought her all sharp angles and harsh lines. But that had been before he'd kissed her and discovered how wrong he'd been. Her air of command hid a raw sexuality that when unleashed had rocked him in ways he'd never imagined.

She jutted her chin in that precise way that meant she'd made up her mind about something. 'It's late.'

'It is.'

'See you in the morning, Dr Albright.'

He stared at her, realising she'd just played the colleague card, putting the boundaries firmly back in place, cutting the attraction off at the knees. Wasn't that what he wanted? Restoration of equilibrium? 'Coffee at seven, Ms Stanfield.'

'Seven it is.'

He ignored the scud of disappointment that gnawed at his gut.

CHAPTER SIX

'SO HAS he put a foot wrong yet?' Poppy held her phone hard to her ear as she took the call in Matt's kitchen while making a late night 'catch-up' sandwich with chicken and salad.

Luke Davies, her favourite anaesthetist, filled her in on Alistair Roland, her competitor in Perth. She'd made the call after coming home from the first choir practice, needing to get her head firmly back in the game of her career rather than letting herself be sidelined by Bundallagong and a man with the smokiest gaze she'd ever encountered.

Not that it mattered that Matt could reduce her to a quivering puddle of need with one gaze, because he didn't want her. Her rational self didn't want him either but her body craved him so badly it sobbed continuously. If past history had taught her anything it was that she doomed relationships, familial and sexual. Even if she had any relationship skills, she couldn't compete with the memory of a dead woman who, unlike her, had made friends with ease and been admired by all she'd met. Matt had made that more than clear three nights ago.

So she'd been very sensible and pragmatic over the last few days, as had he. Whenever they consulted at work they were polite, professional and courteous. No one observing them would have any reason to think they'd once kissed each other senseless. As a result, it was getting easier with every day.

Is that so?

Yes!

You are so deluding yourself.

Luke's voice rumbled down the line, bringing her back to the point of her call. 'You might be in trouble. Alistair's got the nursing staff eating out of his hand.'

'That's not good news.' She opened the fridge, scanning the now considerable contents she'd purchased, and looked for her favourite mayonnaise.

'You wanted facts. I'm just the messenger.'

It was just the sort of information she didn't want to hear. 'Exactly how has he achieved that in such a short time?'

'Sorry, PICU is paging me. I have to go. Hang in there.'

The phone beeped as the call disconnected and Poppy felt the hitch in her gut. She didn't have the XY chromosome to make a predominantly female nursing staff 'eat out of her hand' but she'd always prided herself on being fair. Why didn't that ever seem to count for much?

Frustrated by the report and the paralysis of distance, she snapped her phone shut with one hand, grabbed the mayo with the other and bumped the door closed with her hip.

'What's not good news?'

The mayonnaise and her phone clattered onto the bench as her heart thundered hard and fast. *Matt.* She couldn't be certain how much of her reaction was due to fright and how much was the result of her body's natural response to seeing him.

Her heart hiccoughed.

Question answered.

It was a lot safer to hide behind fright and find indignation. 'First there's the goanna thundering in the roof at 3:00 a.m. whenever a cat disturbs it and now this.' She righted the mayonnaise bottle. 'Didn't anyone ever tell you not to sneak up on a person?'

He gave her a wry smile. 'Sorry. I thought you heard me call out when I came through the door. Is there a problem?'

Never show weakness, Poppy. Her father hadn't been around a lot but when he had, he'd hammered that message home hard, loud and clear. 'No.' *Deflect.* 'Well, there *is* the goanna. It's like an elephant in the roof. How do you sleep?'

His jaw tightened for a fraction of a second. 'The goanna and I have an understanding and you're changing the subject.' His perceptive gaze shone with questions. 'You're wearing a frown as deep as a mineshaft and it isn't goanna related.

Admit nothing. 'I've got a lot on my plate, that's all.'

Matt lowered himself onto the stool by the bench, his manner interested but slightly detached, just like it had been at work ever since they'd buried the entire kissing incident. 'I'm happy to listen.'

'You wouldn't understand.' The words shot out, defensive and self-protective, with the intent of warning him off. Steven had never understood.

Instead of looking offended, Matt just shook his head

slowly as if he felt sorry for her. 'Try me. You might be surprised.'

His long fingers reached out and she watched mesmerised as he snagged a piece of chicken, tilted his head back and dropped it into his mouth. The mouth that had created such delicious havoc the other night and in the process had been branded on her memory for ever.

It had been years since she'd confided in anyone, having vowed never to again after the debacle with Steven. Usually she blocked people with snappy replies and if that didn't work, she crossed her arms. She didn't know if she was overtired, surprised by his interest or just a sucker for *chocolat-noir* eyes, but before she could second-guess her decision, she blurted out, 'I'm fighting for the chief of surgery job back in Perth.'

'Good.'

Indignation roared through her and she slapped mayo and mustard onto wholemeal bread. This was the sort of patronising response she'd got from Steven and the *exact* reason she never opened up to anyone. 'Good? Exactly *how* is it good?'

'You'd be great in that position.'

Surprise barrelled through her, dismantling her righteous anger and leaving behind a trail of confusion. 'Oh, um, thank you.'

Matt raised his brows as he sliced an avocado. 'Now, was telling me that so hard?'

Stop whining, Poppy, and just do the job. 'Yes.'

This time he laughed.

'Seriously, you have no idea.' She pushed her father's and Steven's voices out of her head but thoughts about work took their place. She waged a constant battle— emotionally and physically—to get the same deal as her male counterparts, which meant staying one step ahead at all times. She'd given up so much and she deserved the Perth job, but it was hard to keep fighting for it when she'd been taken out of her own work-place.

His laugh faded. 'Well, you did it, you told me, and life as we know it is still happening, so keep going. What's the specific problem?'

She loaded bread with moist chicken, avocado, thin slices of peppered tomato, fresh basil leaves and lettuce, before adding the top layer of bread and slicing the squares into neat triangles.

'Poppy?'

She knew she was stalling. She pushed one plate towards him and saw intense interest underpinned with support. 'My competitor is currently doing the job, shovelling charm by the bucketload and winning over the staff, while I've been sent up here to languish in the backblocks.'

'Ah.' He bit into the sandwich.

'Ah, what?' She pulled a piece of avocado out from between the slices of bread, her appetite vanishing.

'Who did you upset?'

Her hands hit her hips despite the truth. 'Why do you automatically assume I upset someone?'

'Come on, Poppy, you have to admit that sometimes you have a "take no prisoners" approach that steps on toes.'

She bristled at his criticism. 'You're not perfect yourself.'

'I'm very well aware of that, but right now we're talking about you.' A quiet smile wove through his dark stubble. 'Great sandwich, by the way.'

She leaned against the bench and sighed, partly at her

inability to withstand his smile but mostly because she realised she was totally unable to sidetrack him away from the topic. 'I was covering all bases and I applied elsewhere too and was unsuccessful. News got out and now it's being used against me.'

'But you want the job at Perth City?'

'I do. It's *my job*.' She tapped her chest vehemently. 'I've worked too hard for it to go to some interloper from the east.'

Understanding crossed his face. 'If it helps at all, everyone at the hospital is in awe at how much you've achieved in such a short time and I haven't heard too many grumbles about staff feeling overworked.' His cheeky wink softened his words. 'OK, you might not have the charm quotient like Mr East Coast but you've generated grudging respect.'

Her stomach clenched and she pushed her plate away, virtually untouched. 'Oh, fabulous—grudging respect. That good, huh? That's going to look sensational on my review…not! The only way I can counteract my competition is if I do an equal or better job so I need the staff to like me!'

'That will come with time, Poppy.'

She would have preferred simmering sexuality to this 'father knows best' air and she wanted to shake him. This was *her* career on the line and her voice rose in frustration. 'I don't have time on my side.'

His calm expression didn't change. 'So make it work for you instead of against you.'

'What the hell is that supposed to mean?'

'Be a surgeon at work and a person at play.'

'Play?'

'Yes, Poppy, play. Get out there and go fishing with

the theatre techs, call into the nurses' clothing and product parties, comment on the holiday photos of the clerks, cluck about the cleaner's new grandchild and make sure you show up to drinks at some point *every* Friday night.'

An unfamiliar sensation she didn't want to call panic zipped along her veins and her hand sneaked up to her pendant. 'But that's not me. That's not how I've *ever* done things.'

Matt's gaze showed no mercy. 'Do you really want that chief of surgery job?'

'Hell, yes.'

He grinned. 'And there's the drive we know and love.' He walked round the bench to plug in the kettle. 'Use your drive but redirect it. Show them there's another side to Poppy Stanfield.'

She'd spent years only showing the world the surgeon in charge because it was so much safer. The surgeon had steel-plated armour but the woman buried inside her did not. She crossed her arms in self-protection and her teeth snagged her lower lip. 'What if there isn't another side? What if what you see is all there is?'

'I don't believe that.' A husky edge clung to his voice and the collegiate mentor vanished under the heat-charged words.

Her stomach flipped. Memories of their kisses swirled and eddied around them, mocking everything she'd done to convince herself they were only colleagues. He stood so close to her she could smell the peppermint scent of his shampoo. She wanted his lips on hers, his arms around her waist and his body pressed hard against her, but when she glanced into his eyes, seeking the heat to match his voice, she could only find professional concern and perhaps a hint of friendship.

He doesn't want you. Men don't ever want you. She hated the empty feeling that settled over her and she ducked away from him, briskly covering the uneaten sandwich with cling wrap and covering her own irrational disappointment. 'By the way, I got the all-clear on the house. I'm moving in tomorrow as soon as the new furniture's delivered.'

A muscle close to his mouth twitched and he gave a brisk nod. 'I'm sure you'll be pleased to be in your own space.'

But Poppy read the subtext. He wanted her out and was pleased she was going. For her own peace of mind, she should be pleased too.

At 10:00 p.m. Matt saw the lights go on next door and tried to ignore them. Tried to ignore the fact Poppy was home. He tried to think about work, focus on how they'd both gone out of their way to be polite professionals, but all he could do was picture her in the kitchen, making one of her enormous 'catch-up' sandwiches after a day of grabbing food on the run.

Like the one she'd made him on the night he'd tried so hard not to let his hunger for her take over. The night she'd actually accepted some advice. It had been a good evening and they'd shared a companionable half-hour right up until the moment she'd nibbled her full, lush bottom lip.

He could have taken her right then—in the kitchen, on the bench, against the wall, anywhere. He had no idea how he'd managed not to. How he'd pulled himself back into line so she'd had no clue what he'd been thinking. Then she'd hit him with moving out.

God, he had to stop thinking about her, but the house was too quiet and offered up no distractions. Shadows danced across the walls and the strident, singing cicadas under the deck had gone silent on him. Even the goanna was undisturbed. The sensor light on the deck flickered on, probably triggered by a cat, and a slither of light caught something red behind the barbecue. He squinted and his heart cramped.

Annie's ball. He'd thought he'd collected all her toys but this one had refused to be found, lying in wait to layer on another fresh round of pain. He turned away from the glass and slumped down on the couch. Before Poppy's arrival he'd thought he was finally getting used to the emptiness of the house, if not the silence.

The huge silences were why he hadn't done anything about the goanna, because any sound was at least noise. But post-Poppy he'd realised that just by having another person in the place, even one who argued the point on almost every subject, had lessened the void that had taken over a home. Once it had known so much buzz but now silence had reduced it to a house. Four walls of loss.

Poppy had moved her two red suitcases out three days ago. Three long, quiet and lonely days. His loneliness had shocked him. Since Lisa's death he hadn't wanted company but tonight he ached for it. He'd spent the last three days arguing down every urge to go and visit her. He'd fought off the guise of the friendly neighbour bringing over a house-warming gift, wrestled down the doctor who thought he should 'follow up' on a case, and he'd shut up the eager mentor who kept insisting he should 'check up' and see how she was going with her campaign to warm up the staff.

So far he'd been successful at not going over, but it was consuming every moment of his day. And night. His phone beeped; a blessed distraction, and he read the reminder that flashed up on the screen. *Jen's b'day 2morrow bring food.* He smiled. Jen must have put the reminder in his phone when he'd left it at the nurses' desk.

He knew he hadn't contributed to a staff celebration in a long time and when he did he always bought something from the bakery, but right now, on this particular night, he wanted to make something, and the more he thought about it, the more it seemed like the perfect thing to do. He jumped to his feet and headed into the kitchen. He could only make one thing; a simple, no-cook chocolate slice his mother had taught him when he'd been a kid. She'd called it 'hedgehog'. Opening the kitchen cupboards, he reached to the very back and found a packet of plain biscuits. Amazingly, they were within the 'best before' expiry date.

He started whacking them hard with a rolling pin, enjoying the sensation of doing something normal and everyday. He rummaged through the drawer where Lisa had kept the spices and found cocoa and coconut and added them before opening the fridge for butter and eggs.

A cold, empty space greeted him.

Fresh ingredients? Who are you kidding?

Damn it, he hadn't shopped. *You never shop.* Had he lived in a city, he could have grabbed his keys and hit the supermarket at 10:00 p.m., but he didn't. He slammed the door closed, frustration licking along his veins. For the first time in for ever he'd actually wanted to make something and now he was stymied.

He turned slowly, looking out across the deck, and saw the lights next door were still on. *Poppy.* She'd have butter and eggs and, unlike all his created excuses to visit her, the ones he'd talked himself out of, this one was real. After all, Jen worked really hard and she deserved a birthday morning tea.

Oh, yeah, it's all about Jen's morning tea.

He ignored his sarcastic self. This visit was all about eggs and butter. He strode out of the house, across the garden and straight to Poppy's door, where he pressed the doorbell.

Waiting impatiently, he paced on the small porch. He pressed the bell again, this time holding his finger in place.

'Hang on, I'm coming.'

Poppy's voice sounded deep inside the house, followed by running feet slapping the bare floorboards. A moment later the door opened and Matt swallowed. Hard.

She stood in front of him, her long, black hair cascading over her shoulders like a silk shawl. His eyes followed the line of her hair, across shoulders almost bare except for the slash of the pink spaghetti straps of her camisole top. His gaze skimmed across her round breasts and down to the edge of the top. Here an expanse of tanned belly with the gentle swell of healthy roundedness was met by the band of a skimpy pair of royal-blue pyjama shorts, which clung low on her hips and high on her thighs. And then her legs; her long, long legs stretched on for ever.

He lost the power of speech.

'Matt?' Her blue eyes spun with confusion and concern.

Eggs and butter, remember? 'I need…' The words sounded way too husky. He cleared his throat. 'I need an egg and some butter.'

Her eyes widened and filled with surprise. 'You'd better come in, then.' She turned and walked towards her kitchen, the fabric of her pyjama shorts outlining the sweet curve of her behind.

Heat slammed through him, making him hard, and somehow, with superhuman effort, he managed to keep walking. *Talk about normal stuff.* 'It's to make something for Jen's birthday morning tea.'

'Oh.' She snagged her bottom lip with her teeth and disappointment sounded clear in her voice. 'I didn't know or I would have made something too.'

He stifled a groan. 'Seeing as you're donating the butter and egg, I'll say the hedgehog came from you.'

'You don't have to do that.' She opened the fridge, handing him an egg from the container in the door.

The egg felt thankfully cold in his hot and itchy palm. 'Sure I can. It's not like anyone's going to believe I cooked it.'

She laughed—a deep and throaty sound. 'Yes, but will I want to put my name to it?' She bent over, reaching for the butter, her pants riding up and exposing a glorious expanse of skin.

Heat fired through him, replacing air with all-encompassing need. He dropped the egg.

'Damn it.' He grabbed for a cloth and kneeled down at the same moment Poppy did, her hands filled with paper towel. Their foreheads banged.

'Ouch.' She laughed, her eyes sparkling with life.

Life. She was here, warm, real and, oh, so sexy. For months he hadn't wanted sex but every time he saw her he wanted her. Wanted her badly, and right now he couldn't think of anything else but sex.

Sex with Poppy.

He waited for the gut-wrenching guilt that had pulled him back every time but it didn't come and he didn't understand why but he wasn't going to question it. Poppy was nothing like Lisa and perhaps that was why it didn't feel like a betrayal. All he knew was that his hands burned to cup her bottom and her breasts, his mouth ached to trail kisses along her neck and across her glorious bare skin and he wanted to lose himself in her hair and breathe in her scent of being alive.

He slid his palm along her cheek, tilted her head and kissed her.

Poppy felt his hot lips on hers, felt her body melting, but the protective part of her brain screamed, *Stop!* Somehow she managed to grip his shoulders and pull back. 'Wh-what are you doing?'

Unfocused eyes, loaded with the haze of lust, stared at her. 'Kissing you.'

The words came out thick and hoarse, sending tingling need strumming through her and sucking at the edges of her control. 'What about the hedgehog?'

'I'll buy a chocolate cake.'

She wanted to smile but instead she rose slowly, dignity demanding she speak. 'You've kissed me twice before and pulled back.'

His face tensed and a sad smile curved his mouth. 'I promise you, I'm not going to stop this time. I want to keep kissing you until neither of us can stand.'

She bit her lip as she saw the turmoil of the lust of

now and the pain of the past in his eyes, and felt her own hurt. 'I'm not Lisa.'

His hand played in her hair and he spoke softly. 'This has *nothing* to do with Lisa.'

She didn't know if she should believe him or not. 'Then what is it to do with?'

'Us. This living, breathing "thing" that swirls constantly between us every time we're together, and even when we're not.' His eyes almost pleaded. 'You know what I'm talking about.'

She nodded silently. God help her, she did.

'So we need to have sex to defuse it and bring this "thing" back under control or we're both going to go insane over the next few weeks.' He pressed his mouth to the hollow of her neck.

Stars spun in her head and she clung to rational thought by a thread. 'Sex to defuse it?'

'Exactly.'

She could hardly think straight to follow his so-called logic. She had her own issues to face and she sucked in a deep breath. 'The thing is, I'm not very good at sex.'

'I don't believe that for one minute.' His mouth pressed nipping kisses along her jaw. 'I plan to show you just how good you really are.'

She swallowed hard, trying to stay strong against the delicious rafts of pleasure pouring through her, but she could feel herself slipping under the waves of desire and drowning in their headiness.

His finger tilted her chin so she looked directly at him. 'Sex for the sake of sex. No promises, no regrets, no future and no past, and absolutely no apologies.' His hands gripped her shoulders. 'Are you in?'

Just sex. Nothing more, nothing less.

Why not? It wasn't like she believed in 'happy ever after', and she knew she sucked at relationships and was never going down that torrid path again. She filled her life with work but right now her career hung in the balance, she was a hell of a long way from home and her body constantly hummed for this man. He wanted her body, which was more than any man ever had. Really, what did she have to lose?

Everything and nothing.

She circled his neck with her arms and sank into him with a moan that came all the way from her toes—the bliss of giving in to the longing that had consumed her for days and days. His mouth invaded hers: furnace-hot and with unleashed, potent desire that pulsated through her. She lost herself in his mouth, filling herself with his taste of mint and anticipation, exploring with teeth and tongue. With each foray he met her with one of his own, deepening the kiss, urging her to do the same until all thoughts vanished, the past imploded and nothing existed except his mouth and this kiss.

This time there was no holding back. This time Matt's hand sought her breast, slipping easily under her top, and while his thumb abraded her aching nipple his tongue sabotaged her mouth with bliss. The star-filled night sky had nothing on her body and mind as she lit up, every part of her igniting and burning for his touch. Gasping for breath, she pulled her mouth from his.

He groaned and could barely speak. 'Are you... changing...your mind?'

Her body screamed in protest that everything might come to an abrupt stop right now. 'God, no, but what about protection?'

Matt ran his hand through his hair as an expletive

hit the air. Then he kissed her hard and fast and came up laughing. 'Every hospital house has a medical kit. Where is it?'

Her brain spun with bliss and she fought to think. 'I put it in the bathroom.' He grabbed her hand and tugged her down the hall. 'Matt, it won't have condoms.'

He grinned. 'We're in the middle of nowhere and we have everything.' He flicked the latch and lifted the top tray.

Dipping her hand in, she pulled out a sheet of distinctive square foil wrappers. 'Plenty.'

'Speak for yourself.'

His eyes darkened, sending shivers of anticipation scudding through her. She tugged at his shirt, pulling it over his head, and her eyes feasted on a broad chest, slick with the sheen of the sweat of desire. Desire for her. She could hardly believe it as she reached out her hand, pressing it against hard muscle, feeling his heart thundering against it. 'You're magnificent.'

'So are you.' With a flick of his fingers the three silk-covered buttons of her top opened and he slid the material down her arms to the floor. 'That's so much better.'

His mouth closed over her breast and she cried out with sheer amazement as sensations cascaded over her. Sensations she didn't ever want to stop and she sagged against him as pleasure stole the strength from her legs.

He raised his head from her breast and trailed tantalising kisses back along her breastbone to the hollow in her neck. 'Time to move this to the bedroom. I want room to move and room to see you.' He linked his fingers through hers as he scorched her mouth with another kiss.

She sagged against him. 'I won't make the bed if you keep doing that.'

He tore his mouth away and grinned. 'Can't have that.'

He pulled her down the hall, stopping twice to kiss her. The second time she pressed her back against the wall, her body melting into a puddle of paradise as she clung to him, wrapping her legs around his waist.

He met her moan of need with one of his own and then staggered into the bedroom, carrying her. She fell backwards onto the bed, pulling him with her, never wanting to let him go, needing to feel his hands and mouth on her. She'd never known such rising pleasure, pleasure that tingled and taunted at the same time, and she wanted more of it.

He pulled back to unbuckle his belt and shuck his pants and she whimpered.

A moment or two later, condom in place, he leaned over her, his eyes as dark as rich chocolate, and slowly scanned her body, from her now burning cheeks across her aching pink-tipped breasts and down to her damp panties. He trailed a finger along the lace band before stroking downwards, inexorably slowly.

Her hips bucked as she throbbed with desperate emptiness and delicious promise, both of which were driving her insane. Her fingers gripped his wrist, trying to control his movements, trying to hurry him up before she spun out from unmet need.

'You're so amazingly hot.' His velvet-deep voice floated over her hot, flushed skin and then his mouth took hers for a moment before he slipped his finger under the lace and onto the one place that made her call out his name.

With delicious but maddening touches, he wove a path in ever-diminishing circles until she was beyond coherent thought and begging him. 'Now. Please, now.'

But he didn't do what she asked and instead slipped his finger inside her. She immediately tightened around him as her head thrashed against the pillow, and the tingling zeroed into one intense ball. She tried to pull him down, urge him inside her before she ruined everything, but the ball was soaring through her, sucking her with it, and she let go; let herself be carried into the whirling maelstrom until she was flung out in an explosion of wickedly wondrous and deliciously sweet convulsions that rained through her.

When the last wave ebbed away, leaving her limbs feeling like they were filled with molasses, she gazed up at him, not able to believe her body could do that. She almost sobbed. 'I'm sorry. I've never, that is, I mean…' But words couldn't explain it. 'Thank you.'

'Don't apologise or thank me.' His voice sounded rough and hoarse and he nuzzled her neck, his five o'clock shadow scraping gently on her skin. 'Watching you was almost as good as being there with you.'

She stared at him, studying him hard, trying to find the buried message that she'd done the wrong thing by climaxing before he'd entered her, but all she could see was heat and excitement. Heat for her. *You're so amazingly hot.* Was she? Really?

His tongue found her ear and her post-orgasm bonelessness instantly vanished. Flames licked at her again, building heat, building need, and this time she ached so much it hurt. She wanted to give to him what he'd given to her and she pushed at his shoulders, rolling him onto his back. 'Just lie there, I've got something for you.'

His hands gripped her arms. 'Don't even think about using your hands.'

She laughed and straddled him, her hair making a curtain around their heads. 'I wouldn't dream of wasting this.'

He grinned. 'And you thought you weren't good at this.'

She laughed as exhilaration poured through her and she eased herself over him, marvelling at his beauty. Then she closed her eyes and took all of him, almost crying with relief as he filled her. Moving in a rhythm as old as time, she opened her eyes and saw the combination of wonder and pain etched on his face.

She felt the jab right through to her solar plexus—he was thinking of his wife. *Just sex, no regrets.* She didn't want him to go to that dark place of grief so she kissed him with all she had and then threw her head back, gripping him hard. With more bravado than she felt, she hooked his gaze. 'I'm amazing, remember. Don't let me down now, Matt, or you'll put me in therapy for years.'

Lust drove every other emotion off his face and his hands gripped her buttocks. Rising with her, he drove them both higher and higher, taking them away from everything they'd ever known and hurling them out into a place free of pain and suffering, where they hovered until gravity pulled them back and reality encased them again.

CHAPTER SEVEN

'You look different.' Sarah gave Poppy a long, interrogating look when choir practice finished.

'It's just the hair. You're used to seeing it pulled back at work.' Poppy briskly tapped the pages of her music into a neat pile before sliding them into her folder.

Jen lowered the lid of the piano, smiling. 'No, it's more than that. You've had a secret smile for a few days now and we all know what a secret smile means.'

Poppy schooled her face into a blank expression despite the fact she was really starting to enjoy Sarah and Jen's company. However, she wasn't quite ready to confess to having had mind-blowing and universe-altering sex with Matt every night for a week, although she wasn't totally certain who she was protecting most by staying silent.

She threw her music satchel over her shoulder. 'Well, I did win the slab of beer for catching the biggest fish when I went out with the theatre techs the other day.'

'Oh, yeah, that would do it.' Sarah rolled her eyes and linked arms with Jen. 'I think she's holding out on us.'

'So do I. Especially given there's some new graffiti in the staff toilet that says, "P is a make-out bandit."'

Really? A ridiculous rush of gratitude rushed through her that Matt had actually done that. 'You so know that isn't me. That P has to be Penny Duffield.' Poppy didn't feel too bad about creating that rumour given she'd seen Penny locking lips with her anaesthetic registrar early last Wednesday morning.

Before Sarah could quiz her any more, Poppy's phone conveniently beeped and she checked the text message. *Hungry for food but hungrier for you. M.*

This time nothing could restrain her smile or the rush of anticipatory heat rising in a flush, racing up her neck and burning her cheeks.

'I knew it.' Sarah reached to grab the phone and Jen moved to corner Poppy.

But Poppy had played basketball and could weave and duck, so she used her height to hold the phone high and reached the door before they did. 'Have to go, girls, but great practice.' She stepped out of the door, using it as a barricade. 'Next week I think we'll start an *a capella* piece because the choir has been singing so well. Night.'

Good-natured jeers floated across the car park. 'You know we'll find out.'

'You can't hide for long—this is Bundallagong.'

'I'm not hiding, I'm flying high.' Laughing, Poppy got into her car as she heard Jen mention Damien's name. Hopefully her throwaway line would keep them off the scent for a bit longer.

She could hardly concentrate on driving for excitement. She and Matt didn't see a lot of each other during their workday, and today had been emergency-free so she hadn't seen Matt at all, but they always got together at night. Late at night. Both of them had kept the deal of no past, no future and no regrets. They were living for the moment and ignoring everything else. That was the way it had to be.

What if it could be different?

A tiny daydream started weaving its way through her mind but she immediately applied a wet rag to it, dismissing the thought. Once she'd let dreams of marriage and motherhood derail her and they'd taken her to the bottom of a very black pit. Now she knew that her job was the one thing she could rely on; unlike dreams, her career was concrete. She'd spent years sacrificing everything to climb the career ladder and now she was so close to the top job she couldn't let it go. *Your time here is just a minor detour.*

Five minutes later she parked in her carport and a fizz of surprise washed through her as she noticed that her interior lights were on. As she walked up the short path, her front door opened and Matt stood in the doorway, wearing a white-collared shirt with fine purple and green stripes. He looked neat, pressed and very much the eminent country doctor. But she knew appearances counted for little and the man in those clothes had more in common with his dishevelled hair that covered his collar and brushed his cheeks. Neat on the outside but anguished on the inside.

His aura of sadness didn't seem as dark as when she'd first met him but she wouldn't kid herself that if had anything to do with her. Both of them were conveniently forgetting their real lives for a few weeks and where was the harm in that? This was perfect. *Too perfect?* She banished the traitorous voice in her head, telling herself that with all the depressing news coming up daily from

Perth about how Alistair Roland was 'owning' her job, being with Matt gave her something fun to focus on.

She walked straight into Matt's strong, welcoming arms and breathed in deeply, loving his scent and still not quite believing she could hold him like this whenever they were alone. 'Hey.'

He smiled and kissed her thoroughly.

She lost herself in the pleasure of his mouth and her hands were reaching for the buttons on his shirt when he unexpectedly cupped her cheeks, kissed her on the nose and said, 'I thought we'd eat here.'

She leaned back slightly to focus on his face and at the same time focus on the change in their routine. Every other time she'd been the one to open the door to him and they'd kiss and that led to sex. Always. Granted, he normally arrived at around 11:00 p.m. because one of them had been caught up working, so tonight was unusual because it was only 8:00 p.m. and he was opening the door for her. *Her door.*

She tilted her head. 'By eating here, you mean my fridge has food in it. Food that's required to make something.'

He winked as they walked inside. 'That's part of it but I did bring wine.'

'So you've been waiting here for me to arrive home and cook?' A spurt of irritation washed through her and Steven's voice, which had faded to almost nothing recently, sounded deep and loud in the recesses of her mind. *Is it so unreasonable to expect you to cook?* She stomped towards the kitchen, annoyance growing into anger. She'd had a huge operating day followed by choir practice and the last thing she wanted to do was have to create a proper meal from scratch. The door swung open and the two glasses of white wine and two plates of salad with grilled chicken sat waiting on the bench.

She spun around to see him standing in the doorway, eyebrows raised and a questioning look on his face. Her hand shot to her pendant. 'Oh, God, I'm so predictable, aren't I?'

He stepped in close and kissed her cheek. 'Actually, you're not. Given any other combination of food in the fridge and dinner wouldn't be waiting for you, but the one culinary thing I can do is barbecue.'

'And supposedly make hedgehog, although I've yet to see any.' She smiled, returning his kiss. 'I must remember to always stock meat, then, so you can grill.' She glanced at the tiny kitchen table and then out the window. The sun was dropping fast and the sky was streaked in the vibrant colours of red and orange that Bundallagong offered up almost every night, and that she was coming to love. Right then she lamented the fact she didn't have a deck. 'It's gorgeous out there. Why don't we eat on your deck and enjoy the sunset?'

A tremor of tension rolled across his shoulders. 'The outdoor furniture's covered in bird poop and it needs cleaning. Here's fine and we can enjoy the sunset through the window.' He placed the plates on the set table and then brought over the wine. 'Cheers.'

She tried to shrug off her disappointment. '*Salut.*' She clinked his glass distractedly, realising with a start that every time they'd been together it had been here, at her place. Still deep in thought, she cut into the fragrant and moist chicken and absently put a piece into her mouth. They'd fallen into a routine of him arriving late and usually leaving her bed around 3:00 a.m. to return to his place. She understood that he wouldn't want to have sex in the house he'd shared with his wife but did that preclude social stuff? Deep inside an ache sent out a niggle of distress that she could never compete with a dead woman.

You don't want to compete. This is short term, re-member? You don't want long term. Steven burned you for that.

'Earth to Poppy?'

His words broke into her reverie and she jerked her head up to see his gaze full of questions. 'I'm sorry, what were you saying?'

'I was asking you about your pendant.'

'Oh.' Her hand automatically fingered the tiny dia-monds at the bottom of the fine silver. 'It's a Tiffany P.'

'I gathered that.' He smiled. 'Who gave it to you? Family?'

She thought of her father and his endless array of trin-kets that turned up by express post at birthdays, always with a note explaining why he couldn't visit. 'My father tried to give me a lot of jewellery but not this one.'

He frowned, his dark brows pulling down. 'Your husband, then?'

She flinched. 'My *ex*-husband and, no, he didn't give it to me. If he had, I wouldn't be wearing it.' She stabbed at her salad. 'Why would you assume someone gave it to me?'

'Because I've noticed you always touch it when you're feeling out of your depth.'

She stared at him, horrified. 'I thought we were just having sex, not analysing each other.'

He leaned in towards her. 'We're having fabulous sex

but that doesn't mean I don't notice things. And the fact you're getting defensive means I'm right, doesn't it?'

She took a large sip of her wine, wishing he wasn't perceptive and feeling like she was more exposed than when he gazed at her naked. 'I gave it to myself when I got divorced.'

'New start?' He drizzled balsamic dressing over his salad.

She shook her head. 'More of a reminder to be true to myself. My marriage, unlike yours, was very much a mistake.'

A pensive look crossed his face. 'How so?'

She sighed. 'For all intents and purposes, I married my father.'

He shrugged. 'Was that such a bad thing? I married my childhood sweetheart and statistically that shouldn't have worked either, but it did.'

Childhood sweetheart? It was the first time he'd voluntarily offered up any information about his marriage. She hadn't asked him any more about Lisa because this thing between them didn't mean spilling their guts to each other and dredging up painful memories.

Be honest, you're protecting yourself. You don't want to be held up against the perfect wife and citizen that you can never be. She wanted to put her hands against her ears to drown out the noise in her head or yell *I'm a damn good surgeon*, but both those options would have Matt doubting her sanity.

Instead she said, 'Given my relationship with my father, it was a bad move and not thought out at all. Very unlike me.'

He ran his finger around the base of his wine glass. 'Love is never rational.'

'Now, that *is* handy to know.' She heard the wasp-ish tone that came out automatically to close down the conversation but it only seemed to make him smile.

'OK, point taken. We'll change the subject. Tell me the story behind your name.'

She immediately relaxed. 'Stanfield?' We go back to the Norman Conquest.'

He grinned. 'How very apt. But I meant Poppy.'

Relaxation vanished. 'Of course you did.' She put her knife and fork together on the plate and decided to just blurt it all out and get it over with in one fell swoop. 'My father wanted a son and I was to be named Hugh after him, his father, his father before him and back another three generations. When I arrived and couldn't be Hugh, he gave the naming rights to my mother. She was a florist and my fate was sealed. I was Poppy to Mum, and Dad called me "mate".'

With a pang of immense sadness, Matt thought of his laughing Annie and all his affectionate pet names for her. He felt his brows draw down. 'Mate?'

Her shoulders rose and fell, and resignation rolled off her. 'He wanted a boy and, you know what? I did a damn good job trying to be a son for him. I learned pretty early on that if I played sport, he noticed me, so I became very good at tennis and basketball and I even got to the point where I occasionally beat him at one on one. Things got sticky when I started to develop breasts.' She refilled her glass. 'Around that time he also left my mother for his secretary and finally got the son he'd always wanted.'

Matt's parents had enjoyed a happy marriage so he could only imagine what losing her father's affection must have been like for her. 'Tough to compete with a baby boy?'

'Impossible. Even harder when a second son arrived.' Her usually firm voice cracked for a moment and then steadied. 'I sometimes wonder if it would have been better if Dad had cut himself off completely from my life but instead he'd send money and gifts for every birthday, every academic prize and sporting trophy, leaving me constantly hoping one day he'd actually turn up.'

Matt saw the remnants of a young girl's pain on her face, and caught the moment the steely, determined woman caught up.

She rolled her shoulders back. 'Still, the flip side is that I drove myself to impress him, which got me into medicine, and for *that* I can never have regrets.'

Her words illuminated her work ethic and the constant striving to win, and he realised what had started out as a bid for affection had become ingrained behaviour. 'And your husband was a father figure to you?'

His question shot out on an urge to find out more about the unknown man he actively disliked with an intensity that surprised him. He didn't really expect her to answer it.

Her amazing mouth formed into an ironic pout. 'Not that I was aware of at the time, although the counsellor I saw once post-divorce did point that out.' She took in a quick breath as if gearing up to get something nasty out of the way quickly. 'Steven was fifteen years older than me, divorced and an "empty-nester" with grown-up children. We met when I was a surgical registrar and his brother was one of my first solo procedures. Sadly, his presentation of a perforated bowel turned out to be undiagnosed cancer and he was riddled with secondaries. He died on the table.'

Poppy's fingers laced, her knuckles shining white. 'Perhaps it was my inexperience in dealing with relatives after losing a patient, perhaps it was his charm that was so similar to my father's, I don't know, but we started dating. For a few short weeks he made me feel like the centre of his world and when he proposed, I accepted. We hit the wall within weeks when he realised I wasn't going to be the sort of wife he'd expected. It got angry and ugly, and we divorced.'

Don't let me down: you'll put me in therapy for years. 'The ugly being him telling you that you weren't woman enough for him?'

Her head inclined slightly and then her eyes glittered with resolute grit. 'So, now you know all my sordid details. Aren't you lucky we're living in the moment and me and my emotional baggage will be heading back to Perth in a few weeks?'

He stood up and walked around to her, pulling her to her feet and into his arms, not really wanting to think about the fact her time here was finite. He stroked some inky-black hair back behind her ear. 'Did you happen to see the graffiti that you're a make-out bandit? I think we've managed to unpack and throw out the stuff about you not being woman enough.'

She smiled, a hint of hesitation spinning around her. 'Maybe.'

'Just maybe?' He thought about what they'd done in her bed, how every time the darkness threatened to suck him under she managed to keep him in the moment, and how losing himself in her kept the past at bay in a way hard drinking, exercise or work had never been able to. He wanted their sex to help her too.

'If it's only a maybe then you need to practise more because I know how much you like to be the best at everything.' He knew she could never resist a challenge but just in case he pressed his mouth to her ear, tracing the outline with his tongue, knowing that always made her melt against him and kiss him hard.

Her fingers reached for his belt buckle, unlacing the leather with expert ease, and then bluer-than-blue eyes shimmered with wicked intent. 'Prepare to be exhausted.'

He grinned. 'Sounds good to me.'

'Mr Simmonds, there's a spot on your lung that I want to do a biopsy on.' Poppy sat in a chair opposite the Vietnam veteran, watching his expression carefully.

'Cancer?' He sounded resigned. 'I've been waiting for the thing to catch up with me. Mates I served with have died from it.'

Poppy moved to temper the leap to that conclusion, although most of her agreed with him. 'Or it could be something else, which is why I want to do the biopsy so we know exactly what we're dealing with.'

'This cough's been with me for six months and the antibiotics haven't done a damn thing. Doc, I'm a realist. The war never leaves you and this is just another re-minder.' The sixty-three-year-old's gaze stayed steady.

Poppy was the one who dropped her gaze first. 'I can only imagine what you went through and it probably doesn't come close.'

He shifted in his chair. 'Yeah, but I was one of

the lucky ones. Janice and the girls, they've kept me going.'

Poppy knew Janice from the choir. 'She's a delightful woman, your wife. Being able to share your experiences with her must have helped.'

He shook his head vehemently. 'I've never told her or the girls any of it. Why would I want to taint my home with horrors like that? No, that's what army mates are for. With Janice I can forget.'

His reply astounded her. How could he have been married for thirty-odd years and completely avoided a topic that had had such an impact on his life? 'And it's important to forget?'

'Yeah, love, it is.' His head dipped in reverie for the briefest of moments before he looked back at her. 'So when do you want to put me under the knife?'

Poppy showed her patient the thin, flexible broncho-scope, explained how he would be sedated and how the sample of tissue would be taken. 'I can do it tomorrow. See Sarah on your way out for the paperwork.'

Her pager bleeped loudly. *Need you in Emergency if you're not scrubbed. Jen.*

Mr Simmonds rose from his chair and extended his hand. 'Thanks, Doc. I'll let you get on with your day.'

She walked him to the door and then hurried towards Emergency. Jen met her as she pushed through the Perspex doors.

'Great, I was hoping you weren't in Theatre.'

'What's the problem?'

'There's a child in the resus room with a broken leg and the pain and stress has triggered an asthma attack.'

Poppy pulled on the proffered gown as she walked

towards the room, thinking the break must be pretty bad for Jen to call her. Usually young kids experienced greenstick fractures, which didn't require surgery. 'So, Matt's in with the patient already?'

Jen frowned and shook her head. 'No.'

Poppy's hand stalled on the doorhandle, thinking about her very first day in Bundallagong. 'But he's on his way, right?'

'No. I only called you.'

Poppy felt like she was missing something. 'I'm happy to consult but this is his department and you can't bypass him. You know how he hates that. You have to call him.'

Conflicting emotions played across the nurse's face. 'But the patient's the spitting image of Annie.'

OK, now it was definite. She was totally missing something. 'Who's Annie?'

Jen's eyes dilated in shock. 'You don't know? She was Matt's three-year-old daughter. Lisa and Annie died together.'

His daughter. A wave of nausea hit Poppy so hard she thought she'd vomit on the spot. *Oh, God!* She'd thought it bad enough that he'd lost his beloved wife but she'd no clue he'd lost a child too. Lost so much. No wonder the town had no idea how to behave around him. 'Page him.'

Genuine distress slashed Jen's face. 'But, Poppy, it will kill him.'

She shook her head, knowing that Jen's intentions were good but sadly misguided, and wouldn't help Matt one bit. 'It's not our place to make this decision for him. If he doesn't want to treat the child, that's fine. I can do it. But only he can make that choice.'

'You don't know him like we do or know what he's been through. Sure, he'll bark, but in this case, I know I'm right.'

The unfamiliar exclusion from Jen hit her with a chill, taking her straight back to high school, where she'd never fit in with the girls at school. Part of her wanted to side with Jen, to care for the fledgling friendship she was starting to value, but most of her knew this 'protection mode' was the worst thing in the world for Matt.

She tried to keep her voice even. 'That's very true. I don't know him like you do but this is a hospital, and protocol needs to be followed.'

'Protocol over people?' Jen muttered, before reluctantly picking up the phone.

Poppy bit her lip as she pushed open the door of the resus room, knowing she'd just lost a much-needed ally in Jen and, by default, the Perth job had taken another critical hit. But she'd worry about that later. Right now, she had a patient.

A distressed little girl rested against a bank of pillows with a vaporising mask on her face. Jen had correctly commenced a salbutamol nebuliser but the child was still visibly struggling to breathe, her chest heaving as she tried to force air into constricted and rigid lungs. Her left leg was encased in an air splint and a woman Poppy assumed was her mother sat next to her, holding her hands through the side bars of the emergency trolley.

'Hello, I'm Poppy Stanfield and I'm going to insert an intravenous drip into...' she picked up the chart '...Ashley's arm and give her some drugs that will help her breathe.'

'Thank you.' The worried mother wrung her hands. 'She hasn't been this bad in a long time.'

Poppy nodded her understanding and turned her attention to the little girl. 'Hey, Ashley.' She picked up a cuddle bear that Jen had provided. 'Can you give this bear a big hug for me? He's a bit scared and I know you can show him how to be brave while I put a needle into your arm, OK?'

The little girl's eyes widened in fear. 'Will it hurt?'

'Not as much as your leg does.' Poppy slid the brightly coloured tourniquet around the child's small, pudgy arm and prayed she could find a vein on her first attempt. Surgeons didn't insert IVs very often—that's what anaesthetists were for.

As she swabbed Ashley's arm with alcohol and popped the cover off the cannula, she heard raised voices outside. Matt's rough-voiced yell at Jen didn't surprise her in the least—that she could have predicted. What she couldn't foretell was how he'd react to Ashley.

Matt strode into the room with blind rage, boiling and ready for a fight. First Jen and now Poppy. Not since her first day had she made an arbitrary decision about a patient and he'd thought they'd worked all that out. So much for collegial respect. He couldn't understand it because just lately she'd actually been doing pretty well and gaining ground with the staff, but it was stunts like this that made him wonder if she'd ever learn.

Certainly, after hearing her talk about her father, he totally got why her need to win was so deeply ingrained and work was her world but, damn it, in this instance she knew better. He triaged and if she was required for a consult he called her. It didn't work the other way around.

Poppy's left hip rested on the edge of the trolley and her hair, which caressed his face every night when they had sex, cascaded down her back in a sleek, silky ponytail. She was leaning forward, deep in concentration, and he saw her hand reach for the pre-cut strips of tape on the dressing trolley. The angle of her body blocked his view of the patient but, no matter; he'd see him or her in a moment when he asked Poppy to step down.

'I'm sure you're required elsewhere, Ms Stanfield. I'll take over here.'

She turned and something in her cornflower-blue gaze sent a shiver of disquiet through him. He'd seen those eyes steely with the determination of a woman on a mission, shadowed by the memories of inflicted hurts, filled with the burning fires of lust, and sated with the fog of complete satisfaction. Not once had he ever seen sympathy in their depths, and although it made no sense that is exactly what he saw.

'Ashley, Beth, this is Matt Albright, our emergency specialist. I'm sorry he wasn't here to greet you—there was a slight miscommunication with the nursing staff.' She adjusted the flow of the IV and then moved aside.

His chest tightened so fast air couldn't move in or out of it. A little girl with a riot of blonde curly hair and clutching a hospital bear stared at him through huge, violet eyes.

Daddy, look! I've got a doctor bear with a white coat just like yours.

No. No! This isn't possible. His heart thundered hard and fast, pushing blood through a body that was both icily numb and throbbing in pain. Sweat dripped into his eyes and he blinked rapidly, as if that would help change the image in front of him. But when his eyes refocused, his daughter's double was still there on the trolley, struggling to breathe but, unlike his Annie, still breathing.

'I've started Ashley on IV methylprednisolone.' Poppy pulled a stethoscope out of her pocket and held it out towards him.

He snatched it like a lifeline. 'I'll page you if I need you.'

'I can stay.' The quiet tone of her voice matched her eyes.

His stomach churned and bile seared his gut. God, she knew. How the hell did she know? The town had gone silent, never mentioning the two people he'd loved as much as life itself, and he damn well hadn't told Poppy about Annie because he didn't want her to know. He'd never wanted to see 'that look' in her eyes.

'Get out.' He heard Beth's shocked gasp at the aggression in his voice but he didn't care. No way was he having Poppy in here with pity in her eyes, offering to take over or watching him struggle to keep it all together. Worse still, fall apart. He got enough of that from all the staff.

Her hand crept towards her pendant but stopped short. She rolled her shoulders back and stripped off her gloves. 'Ashley is in excellent hands, Beth, and hopefully the break is a clean one that only requires a cast.' She took a quick step forward and touched Ashley's hand with genuine caring. 'You look after that bear for me, won't you?'

The scared little girl nodded behind the mask as if she was petrified by the thought of Poppy leaving.

At that point Matt didn't know who he hated most—himself, Poppy or the universe.

CHAPTER EIGHT

ALTHOUGH Ashley didn't require surgery, a burns victim from the day before did, and that had tied Poppy up in Theatre until past six. She'd been thankful to have been kept busy because thinking about how much Matt was hurting was just too painful. She hurt too, even though she didn't want to, but the fact he'd never told her about Annie ate at her, making a mockery of everything they'd shared.

What did you expect? The deal you made was no-strings sex. That's want you want, remember, because it's safe.

Except you've been sharing meals and sharing stories, laughing together, and he's become a friend.

The thought chafed like a rash of doubt; hot, prickly and decidedly uncomfortable. Turning her doorhandle, she realised they probably weren't likely to be sharing anything any more. Not when he'd ordered her to leave ED in a voice that could have cut steel, and the look in his eyes had packed the velocity and damage of a bullet ripping through flesh. She stepped inside and the low glow of a lamp greeted her.

'Poppy.'

With a start she turned towards the sound of the deep

but expressionless voice and instantly recognised those familiar and tormented eyes. Surprise became tinged with concern and her heart beat faster. 'Matt? I didn't exp— Are you all—?' But his taut face stole her words, silencing her.

Go for neutral. 'You finished up earlier than I did.'

With his mouth grim and tense, he strode straight to her, his hands gripping the tops of her arms. Silently, he hauled her up onto her toes, pulled her against him, and then took her mouth in a kiss, plundering it with a frenzy close to desperation.

Surprise spun through her at the fact he was there at all, and intensified at the knowledge he still wanted her given what had happened in the ED. She opened her lips under his, wanting and trying to claim her place in the kiss and struggling to find it. She'd never been kissed quite like it, urgent need spinning together with what she guessed was misery.

With a gasp he pulled his mouth away and, still silent, grabbed her hand, tugging her up the hallway to the bedroom. Her feet stumbled at the speed and she should have been angry, perhaps even on one level scared, but all she could feel was his pain roaring through her like a hot wind.

Then his mouth was on hers again, hot, hard and frantic, and she was tumbling back onto the bed. 'This is in the way.' With clumsy movements he pushed her dress upwards but his hands fumbled with her bra.

'Let me do that.' She quickly undid the clasp and unbuckled his belt, and when the clothes were gone, she wrapped her arms tightly around him. Holding him close, trying to give him comfort, and then she kissed him. Softly.

He returned the kiss and for one brief moment his shuttered eyes opened and she saw ragged pain and torment. Her heart cramped so hard she felt the spasm tear clear through her, sending his searing hurt into every cell. She knew then he needed her to be there just for him.

His mouth pressed against her neck, marking a line of ownership as if she might vanish underneath him. Her hands soothed him by caressing his back while he kissed her, but it was like there was an invisible wall between them. But then his mouth took her breast in the way he knew she loved, and her body started to rise on a familiar stream of pleasure. As her mind slipped into bliss and her hips rose to meet his, he entered her, burying himself deeply.

Sensations built, spinning through her, and she wrapped her legs around him, feeling all of him and giving all of herself to him. She touched his face as she always did, seeking his gaze that filled her with joy. But like a man in a trance he looked right through her and all she could see was the reflection of a man trying to outrun his demons. A man who still loved his dead wife.

She swallowed her gasp of hurt. She wanted to wave a wand and change everything. For her. For him. She'd do anything to take away his pain and hurt but she had no power to do that. So she did the only thing she could. She held him tight and sheltered him until he sank with a sob against her, exhausted and spent.

Matt felt Poppy move under him and like a shock of electricity ripping through him he jolted back to earth, realising what he'd just done. He'd taken and not given much in return. He rolled off her, immediately stroking her hair. 'Hell, Poppy. I'm sorry.'

Her clear gaze hooked his and she put a finger against his lips. 'So you got it wrong once. Just don't make a habit of it.' She shot him a cheeky smile. 'Of course, if you're feeling guilty at not totally meeting my needs, you can always buy me flowers, chocolates, champagne and fill my freezer with delicious meals from Lizzie's Kitchen.'

An uncomfortable relief settled over him and he released a breath he hadn't realised he was holding. A breath of thanks. Pressing a tender and appreciative kiss to her forehead, he said, 'Is that all? Nothing in a pale blue box?'

She fingered her pendant. 'No, thanks, I buy my own.'

And that was Poppy to a *P*. Completely independent. Deep down something ached. He knew he owed her a full and detailed explanation about what had just happened but he couldn't do that until he'd made amends. He trailed a finger gently along the curve of her jaw. 'Can I start to make it up to you now?'

Black brows rose. 'What did you have in mind?'

'A neck massage. I know surgeons spend a lot of time looking down, which is tough on the neck muscles.'

She reached out and pressed her hand against his chest, in the same way she always did, with fingers splayed wide. 'Hmm, that might be nice, but I don't have any massage oil.'

Damn. Why hadn't he ever thought of buying some? He covered her hand with his. 'Well, I could massage you in the shower, using soap.'

'Perhaps.' She pouted, her lips slick with the sheen

of desire. 'Surgeons also get aching shoulders and backs.'

He grinned, loving the way this was heading. 'That's very true, not to mention all that standing takes its toll on your legs. I could massage those as well.'

'Could you?' She raised herself up; her pink nipples tightly budded against her creamy breasts. 'An entire body massage? Now, that might just go a long way towards clearing your tab.'

He kissed her with a rush of heat that tangoed with heady affection, and carried her into the shower.

The mattress moved underneath Poppy and a cool draught zipped in around her naked back. Barely awake, she rolled over as part of her brain accepted it was about 3:00 a.m., the time Matt always left her bed. The fact the room seemed lighter didn't really penetrate and sleep quickly pulled her back under. The next moment a shock of white light made her closed eyes ache and she moaned as her arm shot to her forehead to shield her eyes.

'Whoa.' She managed to crack one eyelid open and realised Matt was standing in the room, fully dressed. 'Is it morning?'

His hands circled her wrists and he gently pulled her into a sitting position before sitting down next to her. 'It is. Good sleep?'

She stretched languidly. 'It was an amazing sleep. Best one I've had since arriving.'

'Excellent.' He brushed his lips against her forehead. 'I got up half an hour ago and I've made breakfast.'

Half an hour ago? She could hardly believe it. Thirty minutes meant he'd stayed all night. She'd had her best sleep in—for ever, and he'd been in her bed all night.

She didn't want to let herself connect any dots about those two events but already her mind was doing it. 'Is there coffee with breakfast?'

'There is.' He tossed her a pair of shorts and a T-shirt.

She tugged the top over her head. 'Can't I have it in bed, seeing you've woken me up at...' she squinted at the clock '...stupid o'clock?'

'No. Breakfast is at my place.'

His place? She pulled up her sagging jaw as he walked out of her room. They never spent any time at his place. She fell into her shorts, wondering what was going on, and stumbled into the bathroom.

Five minutes later she slid, grumbling, into a chair at Matt's kitchen table and found herself in front of a steaming mug of coffee. 'You'd better have food as well as coffee.'

'Are you always this delightful first thing in the morning?' Matt sat down next to her, coffee in one hand and a photograph album in the other. 'I'm short on fresh food but I'll buy you something from the bakery on the way to work.'

'You're always short on fresh food because you never shop. Why are we here when I have fruit and yoghurt at my place?'

'Because my coffee's better and I need to show you this.' He put the album on her placemat and opened it up. A little girl with eyes the colour of grape juice stared up at her. 'I'd like you to meet my daughter.'

Her heart hiccoughed and she touched his hand as she continued to turn the pages of the album looking at photos of a loving wife and mother, a proud and loving husband and father, and a child they both clearly adored.

She wondered about that kind of love; a love that en-compassed everyone in the family, the sort of love she'd never known. A bright green streak ricocheted through her. What sort of a shocking person was she to be jealous of a dead woman and child?

One that wants the same thing?

No. Thoughts of the dark days of her childhood and her marriage shored up her momentary lapse.

'All those curls. She's gorgeous.'

'Yeah.' He ran his hand through his hair, the strands falling back and masking his face, and then his body shuddered. 'Annie and Lisa died on a beach in Samoa when a tsunami struck. I was spending the day at an inland village and survived.'

She immediately wrapped her arms around him, resting her forehead on his, wishing she could take away all his pain and knowing she couldn't touch it. 'I can't even imagine what this is like for you.'

He absently kissed her cheek. 'I know.'

She needed him to really understand. 'I had no clue you had a daughter until yesterday when Jen and I argued over why she hadn't called you to the ED.' She tried to keep the hurt out of her voice. 'Why didn't you tell me, Matt?'

He shrugged. 'Perhaps I wanted *one* person not to define me by what I'd lost. One person who could stare me down, argue with me and treat me just like any other bloke.'

She bit her lip and tried not to tear up, tried to be the same person she'd been yesterday. 'I can argue the point.'

A quiet smile tugged at his lips. 'You can, and you do it very well.'

She thought of Mr Simmonds and how he'd never told his wife about the war because he didn't want to have to think about the horrors he'd been through when he was with his family. A shaft of clarity hit her and she realised why Matt was showing her photos of his family in his house and not hers. 'I still plan to argue with you.'

'I hope you do.' He dropped his head into her hair and sighed. 'Poppy, about last night. Seeing Ashley, who looks so much like Annie, and realising that you knew about her, well, I lost it. I haven't lost it in a long time. I'm truly sorry.'

She cupped his jaw and raised his head to hers, fighting an irrational sadness about her role in all of this, which was crazy. She had no reason to feel sad because she wasn't sticking around. She'd learned a long time ago that work was safer then relationships with all their inherent pitfalls and she knew Matt certainly wasn't looking for one. Yet she couldn't quite shake the feeling that perhaps together they could have something more. 'It's OK, I get it. Me and my house are a place for you to come and forget.'

Matt raised his head slowly and met Poppy's eyes filled with tacit understanding and something else he couldn't define. 'You're an amazing woman, Poppy.'

A ripple of tension shot along her mouth before she smiled. 'That's me. Brilliant surgeon and sex goddess.'

The quip reassured him that things hadn't changed between them, that their loose arrangement would continue while she was in town and she wasn't going to go all touchy-feely on him and want him to bare his soul even more. That was the beauty of Poppy: she didn't do emotions very well, either. With her he could still pretend his life hadn't been turned upside down and pulled sideways, and when that got too hard, he lost himself in her.

She drank more coffee. 'Have you been back to Samoa?'

He shook his head. 'I stayed there for a few months after it happened and then I thought it was time to come home.'

'How's that working for you?'

He didn't want to analyse that at all so he gave her the bare minimum. 'I think I mentioned the initial drinking binge but that's long over and now, well, I get through each day. I know I can treat children again, even ones who look like my daughter, so that has to be an improvement, right?'

A thumping noise sounded from the roof and Poppy's eye's rolled. 'And yet you let Rupert live in your roof?'

Unease shot through him that she was way too close to the truth. 'Why are you so obsessed by the goanna?'

'I'm not. I'm merely pointing out most people wouldn't want something like that living in their roof, causing damage to the house.' She stood up, taking her cup to the sink. 'Are you sure living here is the right thing for you?'

He gripped his coffee mug, hating that she'd just asked the question he often asked himself. 'Of course I'm sure. This is my home.'

Two small creases appeared at the bridge of her nose. 'This house or this town?'

'Both,' he said, but knew he lied. He stood up, knowing the exact way to cut this conversation off at the knees. 'You'd better hit the shower or you're going to be late for work.'

She yelped as she caught the time on the clock. 'Oh, hell, is it really seven-thirty? I've got pre-op consults in fifteen minutes.'

He saw a blur of colour, heard her feet on the bare boards and then the door slam. He grinned. 'Poppy has left the building.' He went to close the photo album and saw Lisa's face smiling up at him. He braced himself for the sear of guilt—guilt that he was still living, guilt that he'd found pleasure with another woman—but it didn't come. He released a long breath, left the page open and headed to the shower.

Sweat poured off Poppy as she gesticulated, controlling the choir with her arm movements, and backed up by her silent mouthing of the words. The clear, true sound of *a capella* rolled over her as the words of 'Amazing Grace' soared along with such a wave of feeling that she felt tears sting her eyes.

With her fingertips touching, she slowly drew her hands apart, holding the last note until she fisted her hands to indicate 'stop'. She grinned at the women's awestruck faces. 'Yes! You really did sound that fantastic. Well done. I think Sarah has posters about the concert she'd like you to put up so please take one with you before you leave, and on that note I'll call the formal part of choir over for the night. There's the usual tea and biscuits if you can stay.'

Shrieks of delight followed with the choir members breaking to give each other high-fives and Poppy turned as Sarah's hand touched her shoulder. 'Amazing.'

'Grace.' Poppy smiled.

'Take a compliment, woman!' Sarah hugged her. 'They're going to rock the town at the concert.'

'You mean the five people who might actually come out on a Sunday afternoon.'

'Yeah, well, there's that, but Justin's selling tickets at the surgery with the odd bribe, and I heard Matt Albright's reply to a recovering Daryl Jameson when he was trying to thank him for saving his life. He said that all the thanks he needed was Daryl attending the concert.'

Poppy groaned. 'These women deserve more than a pity audience.'

'You worry about the music and let us locals get the audience.'

Us locals. An odd feeling settled in Poppy's belly, and she tried to shake it off. It was ridiculous that she was letting two little words, two absolutely accurate words, make her feel uncomfortable. Sad almost. It didn't make a lot of sense—in fact, it made none at all because it wasn't like she planned on staying.

You're just tired and emotional. This is nothing a good sleep won't fix. Remember, this is a godforsaken place that's just a blip on your career radar.

A small voice protested. *The sunsets are amazing. So are the people.*

People like Matt.

Her stomach flipped, scaring her, and she dragged her mind back so fast from the man who was turning her world upside down that she risked mental whiplash. It was time to focus on the choir.

She'd met some incredible women out here, women whose lives were far from perfect but they kept going, trying to improve their situation and those of their families. Local or not, she wanted to honour them and be involved.

'I want this concert to be a success. How about we have a planning meeting at my place now? I got a hamper sent up from Perth yesterday with a fabulous Margaret River white wine, Swiss chocolate and a gorgeous runny Camembert that needs to be eaten.'

Sarah laughed. 'First of all you give me the "no-sex" talk and now this. Are you asking me out on a date?'

She smiled, enjoying the teasing. 'You found me out.'

Jen wandered over. 'Found out what?'

Things had been a bit strained between Jen and herself since the incident in the ED and perhaps this was a way of building bridges. 'Drinks at my place now—can you come?'

Jen visibly started. 'Really? OK, why not? Can I catch a ride with you?'

'Sure. We can ask Janice Simmonds to lock up, can't we?'

Sarah nodded. 'Janice will do anything for you now you've cured Harry. Your eyes were like saucers when you saw that sprouting pea in his lung.'

This time Poppy high-fived. 'Well, it was a pretty amazing find and so unexpected, but in a good way.' And not just for Harry Simmonds. The uniqueness of the case meant it had made it into the 'odd spot' in the Eastern papers and the Royal College of Surgeons had asked her to write it up for their journal. It was win-win for the patient and for herself, as well as a shot across the bows to Alistair Roland, William and the board. They might have sent her to the outer Barcoo but she was still a force to be reckoned with.

Sarah kept them entertained on the quick drive home with a story about a very tired Justin being called out of an antenatal clinic to stitch up a nasty wound when the patient had lost a battle with a bush saw. 'He was stitching John Ledger's hand.'

'I don't think Poppy's had the pleasure of meeting John,' Jen chimed in.

'If you think most of the blokes in this town are tough then John is reinforced steel. Anyway, Justin's going through the motions, asking all the important questions, but instead of asking John when he last had a tetanus injection, he asked the question he'd been asking all afternoon at the pregnancy care clinic, which was, 'When did you last have a pap test?''

Jen started to giggle. 'Poor Justin.'

'John gave him one of his famous "you're a moron" looks and said, "At the same time I had my last tetanus shot." John went straight from the surgery to the pub and Justin's never going to live it down.'

The laughs continued as they shared embarrassing work stories and Poppy poured wine and Jen opened chocolate and cheese.

'OK, how are we going to sell this concert as a "must attend" event?' Poppy tapped a pen against a note pad. 'Offer food?'

Jen sliced the cheese. 'Serve beer and the men will come.'

Sarah sat forward, wine glass in hand. 'Poppy, remember your first week here when you operated on the head of transport for the mining company?' She clarified, 'The bowel obstruction.'

Poppy nodded as his name came to her. 'Ed Papasoulis?'

'That's him. The miners who "fly in, fly out" get collected and taken to the airport. I'm sure with a word to him the bus could be early that day and come via the concert. It's only going to be half an hour and it would double our audience. Any unsupportive husbands who weren't planning on coming will be there on company time, and have the added benefit of being blown away by their wives' performances.'

Poppy stared at her. 'I'm in awe of your scheming.'

Sarah shrugged and gave her a grin. 'Perhaps I'm learning from you. By the way, great sound bite and visual on the Perth news the other night about Harry. So how's the battle for the Perth job going?'

'I wish I knew. It's just so hard being this far away and not being able to see my opposition in action and lobby.'

'He can't see you either so that levels the playing field a bit, doesn't it?' Jen remarked as she sipped her wine.

The support in the words both surprised and reassured Poppy. 'I guess I never really thought about it that way. Thanks.'

'No problem.' Jen paused for a moment. 'Listen, Poppy, I'm sorry about the other day with Matt. The thing is, just lately he seems to be coping better, looking less tormented and even cracking jokes and smiling, and I didn't want seeing Ashley to bring the trauma back again and send him backwards.'

An apologetic look touched her face. 'But you were right and I was wrong. He managed to hold it all together but I hated watching him have to do it.'

Poppy thought about how he'd fallen apart in her arms a few hours later. 'It was a tough day all round and no choice was easy, but it had to be his choice.' She offered the nurse a chocolate. 'Truce?'

Jen frowned. 'There was never a war, Poppy, we just differed in opinion. Friends can do that, you know, and then they talk it out.' She popped the ball of rich pra-line chocolate into her mouth and murmured a sound of delight. 'Oh, my God, Sarah, you have to try these.'

Sarah chose a chocolate and joined Jen in equal rhap-sodising about the taste and texture, and Poppy leaned back and watched.

Friends. She realised with a start that these two strong women really did consider her a friend. The feeling settled over her like a new pair of shoes that fitted but would become truly comfortable with some extra wear. She was looking forward to it.

The front door opened with its usual squeak and Jen and Sarah looked up as Poppy's gut clenched. *Matt.* She'd been on such a high after the choir practice and enjoying herself with the girls, she'd forgotten to text him.

He walked in, talking. 'I thought we— Ladies, good to see you.'

The change in his conversation was almost seamless and if Matt was surprised to see Sarah and Jen, his face didn't seem to show it. He held up a bottle of wine. 'I brought wine for the choir meeting.'

Shock rendered Poppy speechless but Sarah stood up and accepted the bottle with a smile. 'Thanks, Matt. This is really thoughtful and will add to our spur-of-the-moment meeting. By the way, didn't know you were psychic.'

He didn't skip a beat. 'It's one of my many skills. I'll

leave you girls to it. Have a good night.' He closed the door behind him.

Sarah spun around with a squeal and pointed straight at Poppy. 'You are so having sex.'

Jen punched her gently on the arm and beamed. 'No wonder Matt's been looking better lately.' She looked at Sarah. 'How did we miss this?'

Sarah sat down. 'Because Poppy is cagey.'

Poppy tried to deny it, shaking her head. 'I'm not cagey and I'm not having sex.'

Sarah crossed her arms. 'The game's over, Poppy, and now it's time to spill. But before you do, can I just say thank you?'

'Thank you? I don't understand.'

'Matt and you as a couple—it's just so great after what he's been through.'

A ripple of panic set off through her and Poppy's hands flew up like stop signs. 'No, please, don't make that leap. I've been married once and never again. This is just sex. I'm only here for a few more weeks and, like you said that night in the bar, why not have some fun? See, I took your advice.' The words spoken with true conviction sounded strangely hollow.

Sarah frowned. 'Does Matt know?'

'It was *his* idea.' She moved to reassure their worried expressions, finding it harder than expected. 'Neither of us wants anything permanent and he still loves Lisa. We're both adults who've gone into this with eyes wide open. There's nothing for you to be concerned about.'

Liar.

The creases in Jen's brows faded slightly. 'Well, you have to admit, he's been a lot happier, so that's a good thing, right?'

Sarah didn't look quite so convinced but she smiled and leaned forward. 'Just sex, eh? So how good is it?'

Poppy leaned back, raised her glass to her friends, unable to stop a wicked smile racing across her face. 'Let's just say good is a far too prosaic adjective to describe it.'

CHAPTER NINE

POPPY kicked up from the depths of the water hole, breaking the surface, and felt Matt's arms wrap around her. She leaned back against him and stared up at the clear Outback sky. A strange feeling washed over her and she realised with surprise that this was what happiness felt like.

A while later, she lay in the shade cast by the massive, red-walled gorge, soaking in the unexpected coolness, when a mere forty steps away the sun was unrelentingly hot. 'It's so amazing that in the middle of all this arid, red-rocked, gibber-plain nothingness, there are ferns and a permanent water hole.' She rubbed her arms, flicking off the water from her swim, and laughed. 'I'm almost cold. How weird is that?'

Matt wrapped a towel around her shoulders. 'The Outback has its secrets, you just have to open yourself up to them.'

'And here I am.' She gave him an arch look. 'Although I thought the guy who asked the girl out did everything.'

He grinned. 'Division of labour. I drove and you arranged the picnic.'

She smiled against a looming frown. 'I'm not sure

that's actually a fair division, considering driving here happened on your day off and yesterday I had to shop and then put the food together.'

He winked. 'Yeah, but it made you finish work a bit earlier. Besides, you needed a day off and I've wanted to bring you out here for ages.'

She flicked him with the towel, half in jest and half serious as the scars of her marriage reddened. 'This week I've been home by eight three nights and no paper-work. I really think I've broken the back of the waiting list and things are getting more manageable and into a routine. Besides, you're the one who told me to go fish-ing and accept invitations to clothing parties, so today was my first totally free day.'

'How dumb was I? Still, that advice was before I got you into bed.' He kissed her on the nose. 'If you asked today, I might tell you something different.'

'I'm not so sure about that.' She looked hard into his eyes, trying to read more. She could see affection but it ran into something else. Something that prickled at her. 'All I'm saying is that I came here with a job to do, and I'm getting it done.'

'And all I'm saying is that *balance* in life is good.' He stretched out next to her. 'Your phone doesn't work out here and doesn't it feel good not to be obsessively checking emails?'

A defensive flicker clenched her gut. 'I don't obses-sively check emails.'

He cocked a knowing brow.

'OK, but to be fair, I've been sending William bi-weekly reports. How unreasonable is it to expect a reply?'

'Poppy, he holds the power in this so accept that he's toying with you and make it work for you.'

All her fears collided. 'This is my career you're so casually talking about. My life.'

He sighed. 'I know it's not easy for you to take advice but if I've learned anything in the last year and a half it's that life isn't all about work.'

She thought about how her father had consistently let her down, and how Steven had zeroed in on her need to be loved, turning it into a battlefield of 'you change and then I'll love you'. Now Matt was hinting along similar lines. The one constant in her life, the one safe thing that didn't let her down, was her career. 'And I've learned that my work is far more reliable than anything else.'

He opened his mouth to reply but she didn't want to spoil the day by arguing any more about work or work-loads so she leaned over and pressed her mouth against his, kissing him deeply and hoping that was enough to distract him. 'Thanks for bringing me out here.'

He stroked her hair as she rested her head against his chest. 'You're very welcome. Walker's Gorge is always worth the drive. When I was a kid, Mum would choose the beach for picnics but Dad and I loved it out here. It was a favourite with Lisa's family, too. I remember getting into serious trouble when I was five after I pushed her into the water hole.'

Five! She could scarcely believe it. 'You really were childhood sweethearts.'

He crooked his free arm behind his head. 'It's hard to think of a time when she wasn't in my life.'

'What about uni?'

'Lisa came to Brisbane with me.'

It was spoken so casually, as if it was totally un-

remarkable that two people had lived all their lives together, but Poppy's surprise swooped to her toes. Had
they never been apart until her death? 'So you were at
uni together?'

'No, Lisa didn't want to go to uni. She was an artist
and made the most amazing jewellery. She worked in
the office of a law firm and made jewellery at night.'
His mouth curved into a smile full of pleasant memories.
'We had a tiny flat with bookshelves made out of bricks
and wood, beanbags for furniture, and it was decorated
with Lisa's artwork. Her parents weren't happy about
any of it and would visit often, mostly so her father could
give me a really hard time about how I was a kept man
because Lisa was earning more money than I was as a
student.'

His chest rose and fell under her cheek. 'The moment
I qualified we got married, and I took great delight at
outearning her so she could quit her job and do jewellery
full time. When Annie arrived, we moved back here and
she cut back the jewellery to commission pieces only
because she loved being a stay-at-home mum and being
involved in the town, volunteering.'

He'd never talked so openly and Poppy knew she
should be pleased for him that he'd now reached a place
in his grieving where he could do this, only the green
monster that had been slumbering of late raised its head.
Lisa had been family-oriented and naturally giving, everything *she* wasn't.

*Does it matter? It's not your future. Your future is
Perth.*

Is it? A hollow feeling filled her gut. The words
so easily spoken when they'd first started their affair
were getting harder and harder to believe, but her heart

knew the alternative wasn't an option. Having it all—
career, marriage and kids—was a big-time con and she'd
learned that the hard way.

If he'd noticed her silence he didn't show it. 'If I'm
honest, Lisa's choices made my life a lot easier because,
given the hours I sometimes work, coming home to an
oasis of calm was a gift.' He tensed. 'Ironically, it was
her push to go to Samoa that changed everything.'

'No one was to know a holiday would end like
that.'

He shook his head. 'We weren't there on holidays.
Lisa had read about an organisation working with indig-
enous women to help them achieve sustainable futures
and thought she could offer her skills and knowledge
about turning crafts into income. She had it all worked
out: we'd go for half a year and I could do medicine
while she did business models.'

Poppy propped herself on an elbow and thought
about how he'd mentioned staying in the Pacific for a
while after the tsunami. 'So you stayed and fulfilled her
vision?'

He frowned and the sadness that had left him returned. 'I stayed because I couldn't leave. I tried to leave,
believe me, but I just couldn't separate myself from the
island because it meant I had to accept Lisa and Annie
were gone. Initially, I was part of the relief effort and
the frantic pace kept the real world at bay, but once the
Red Cross realised who I was, they pulled me out of
the field because, as the paperwork described it, I was
one of the victims.' His chest heaved. 'God, I hate that
word.'

'So don't use it.' She pressed her hand to his chest,
wanting him to see himself in a new light. 'You're

someone directly affected by the event and it changed the direction of your life irrevocably. It's not OK that it happened but it doesn't make you a victim.'

Matt traced a finger down Poppy's cheek, marvelling at her inherent strength. 'I like that reframing.'

'It's yours. What brought you back to Bundallagong?'

'Time, and Lisa's father eventually came over and said the town needed me back.'

'Did you want to come back?'

He shrugged. 'I had to do something and coming home was at least familiar. Same town, same job.'

'Same house.' She wrinkled her nose. 'I think it must be unbelievably hard to try and live the same life you were living two years ago but without Annie and Lisa. I don't think it's really helping, is it?'

Her words echoed harshly yet truthfully in his head. He thought of the town's tentativeness around him, of how the only place he'd ever felt close to normal was at work and how he now hated a house he'd once thought was the only place he'd ever want to live.

'Nothing I do will bring them back so it really doesn't matter what I do or where I live.'

A shot of white anger sparked in the depths of her eyes, shocking him. 'That's not true. You have choices, Matt. You don't have to try and live the life you had before they died but why not finish the chapter you were living in when the tsunami hit? Lisa had a vision that she can no longer achieve but you can make it happen in her name.'

Fury, powerlessness and panic skittered through him. 'I know nothing whatever about jewellery, Poppy!'

She sat up straight, her face both earnest and irritated. 'But you probably know people who do, and if you don't, you can find them. Who you actually know are the people in this town who loved and cared for Lisa and Annie, so start there. Do some fundraising and create a foundation in their name so the work can be funded long into the future.'

A foundation? He tried to shrug off the thought, cross that Poppy was being her usual steamroller self, but it insisted on taking a tenuous hold. Why hadn't he thought of something like that? *Because the time wasn't right and you weren't ready for it.*

Was he ready now? The more he thought about it, the more the idea appealed. A foundation would do two special things—remember Lisa and help in a way she would have totally approved of.

And of all the people to think of this perfect idea, it had been Poppy, who hadn't even known Lisa. In a way it connected them and he found that oddly consoling. A tide of mixed emotions poured through him and when he spoke, his words came out roughly. 'Have you always been this damn bossy?'

She blinked and then a slow smile strolled across her cheeks before smouldering in her eyes. 'Yes. Bossy and in this case absolutely right.' She rummaged in her backpack. 'I'm sure I've got a pen and paper in here and you can start brainstorm—'

He shot his hand out to touch her arm. 'It's all about balance, remember. I can and I will do that later, on the long drive back. But right now we're on a day off and...' He pulled her into his arms, nuzzled his face against her neck and smiled as she relaxed against him. His blood hummed when he heard her delicious moan of consent.

'My dad does that to my mum.'

Poppy's eyes flew open in wild and shocked surprise as Matt's mouth trailed kisses along her collarbone while his hand caressed her left breast. She frantically leaned sideways to hide her partial nakedness and try and see who was talking. Matt almost toppled forward into the newly created space.

A little boy, who looked to be about five or six, stood in front of them, and she struggled to find a coherent reply as she pulled the shoulder strap of her bikini back into place. 'D-does he?'

The child gave a serious nod.

Matt, having righted himself, now squatted at eye level with the child, a smile on his face. 'Well, that's good to know because it means he loves your mum.'

Love? Panic and joy stalled Poppy's heart for a moment before common sense prevailed. Matt was merely explaining why he'd been more than just kissing her, in terms a child could understand.

'They close the bedroom door.'

'Obviously not always,' muttered Matt, throwing her a look that combined laughter with chagrin. 'I'm Matt. Who are you?'

'Lochie, and I five.'

'Five, hey? That's getting big. And where did you come from, Lochie?' He shielded his eyes with his hand and peered beyond the child and down the stony river bed, looking for people.

The little boy pointed behind him. 'There.'

Poppy, now decent, scrambled forward, wondering why this child was alone in the middle of nowhere. 'Where are Mummy and Daddy?'

'I runned here first.'

Matt's mind was obviously going to the same place

as hers and he put his hand out to the little boy. 'How about we go back the way you came and meet them? Because even though you know where you are, Mum and Dad don't.'

Lochie shrugged. 'OK.'

Poppy grabbed their towels and stuffed them inside the backpack. 'I'll come, too.'

Matt nodded, his face full of concern. 'Good idea. There are two water holes in this area so I've got no clue which one his parents are heading for. The track, if you can actually call it that, divides. Best bet is to return to the car park and we either meet them on the way or we wait there until they come back to sound the alarm.'

She touched his arm. 'Am I missing something about an Outback childhood or is the fact he's separated from his parents really dangerous?'

'No, you're right, but not everyone realises the dangers in this place until it's too late.'

They started walking and Lochie immediately streaked out in front, which was obviously what had got him separated from his parents in the first place.

Poppy called out, 'Hey, Lochie, slow down,' but the little boy didn't alter his pace.

Matt sprinted up to him, catching him by the back of his T-shirt, and Poppy caught up to them just in time to hear Matt say, 'Want to play a game, mate?'

Lochie's eyes lit up. 'What is it?'

'You stand between Poppy and I, and hold our hands. We all walk together counting out loud, and something special happens on three.'

'OK.' The child's warm hand slid into Poppy's as Matt mouthed over his head, 'We swing on three.'

Poppy knew Matt the lover, Matt the grieving

widower and the professional doctor, but this was the first time she'd seen the father in him. Deep down inside her an old, faded and discarded dream moved.

'Let's go.' Poppy started walking briskly to push away the unsettling feelings. *Chief of Surgery is what you want and where you belong. You gave up the dream of motherhood a long time ago. Work is far more reliable than men.* 'One, two…' she gripped Lochie's hand firmly in her own to avoid any slipping '…three!' Her arm swung forward, as did Matt's, and Lochie's legs swung sky high.

As the child's feet touched the ground again, he gave a whoop of delight. 'Again.'

Poppy laughed at his joy and looked across at Matt, knowing he would have done this very thing with Lisa and Annie, and a combination of concern for him and envy for herself sat heavy in her gut.

His expression was a revelation. Instead of the raw pain she'd seen so often in his eyes, his dark gaze held warm delight with a glimmer of resigned sadness. Sadness she knew would understandably stay with him for ever in some shape and form when he remembered his beloved daughter. Seeing him in action with Lochie, she knew he'd been a wonderful father.

The dream shifted again, tugging hard, morphing into something tangible and real. *You, Matt, a child on a picnic out here.* It tempted her so much that it terrified her. This time she deafened it with a loud yell of 'One, two…*wheeeeee*!'

The sun was dropping low in the sky and the air temperature dropped with it. Matt jogged back from the second water hole track, now seriously worried. He could see Poppy in the distance, wrapping Lochie up in one of the towels to keep him warm. Where the hell were his parents?

Relief filled Poppy's eyes when she saw him. 'Are they on their way back?'

'I didn't find them.'

Her face blanched and he gave her arm a squeeze. 'It's time to contact the police.' He leaned into the truck and got onto the radio as he heard Lochie asking for food.

'What about a lucky dip?' Poppy sounded overly bright as she opened the top of her backpack. 'Stick your hand in there and see what you can find.'

Lochie looked sceptical but Matt smiled, knowing Poppy had a secret stash of food in that pocket of her backpack. She had a natural affinity with children, which had been another surprise to him. It shouldn't have been. He'd learned over the past weeks that once people got past the smoke and mirrors of her no-nonsense, crisp façade that she hid behind, they found a woman with a huge capacity to give.

'Chocolate!' Lochie held up the distinctive purple-foiled bar.

'Jack, it's Matt Albright. We're at Walker's Gorge with a five-year-old and his parents are missing. Vehicle has New South Wales plates. We've been back at the car park for well over an hour and I've walked the two tracks the little bloke said he'd been on but there's no sign of them.'

'Five-year-olds are not that reliable, Matt.' The experienced police officer took the registration number and went on to suggest he break into the vehicle for any clues.

Cursing central locking, he yelled to Poppy and Lochie. 'We need a big rock to break a window.'

'Now, that's not going to be hard to find.' Poppy took two steps, picked one up and threw it through the driver's side window.

'You're really bad!' Lochie threw himself at Poppy's legs and she immediately bent down. 'Sweetie, I'm sorry but we need to see if Mummy or Daddy left a map or a plan of where they were going and they're not going to be cross, I promise.'

'I want Mummy.' The small boy's wail rent the air.

'I know you do, Lochie.' She gave him a quick hug and then opened the car door, carefully brushing away the shards of glass with a towel before looking for any identifying information.

Matt hung onto the radio, waiting for Jack. 'Have you found anything, Poppy?'

She held up a National Parks brochure. 'There's a map of the park and both water holes have been highlighted.'

'Matt.' Jack's voice crackled down the line. 'Car's registered to a Lance Wilkinson and we've just had a report that a personal location beacon's been activated in the area. Do you have a map?'

He leaned over and grabbed the laminated and de-tailed hiking map he always carried when he came out here. 'Got it.'

'Find your location. On the west side of the car park there's a rough side track that heads along the ridge. The GPS in the PLB is coming from there. You can get in by vehicle if you drive to Koonunga picnic ground.'

'How the hell did they end up there?' But it was a rhetorical question because to an inexperienced walker all scraggly gum trees and red rocks looked the same and taking the wrong direction was sadly far too easy. 'We're on it, Jack.'

He turned to call Poppy, only to find her sitting in the dirt by the other vehicle, cuddling a sobbing Lochie. Her right arm held him close and her left hand stroked his hair while the little boy clutched a well-loved soft toy bear she must have found for him in the car. Her dark hair rested against the boy's jet locks.

Mother and child. Poppy as a mother. The image stuck him hard in the solar plexus. He had to clear his throat before speaking. 'We've got co-ordinates, hop in.'

Half an hour later, after bouncing along a rocky escarpment no one in their right mind would call a road, and using their GPS, Jack's guidance and their eyes and ears, Matt stopped the truck for the fourth time and hopped out. Bringing his hands up to cup his mouth, he yelled, 'Cooee.'

Then he listened. He'd been straining to hear anything for so long that at first he thought the returning 'cooee' was his own voice.

'Did you hear that?' Poppy's face filled with hope.

He called again, and this time Lochie and Poppy joined in.

A male voice replied, 'Cooee. Help us.'

'We're on our way.' Matt grabbed the medical bag and was starting to walk in the direction of the voice when a bearded man, supporting a woman, stumbled into the clearing.

'Mummy, Daddy!' Lochie pulled out of Poppy's grasp and ran to them.

'Thank God, Lochie.' The woman sobbed out her

child's name as she was lowered to the ground, gripping her left arm close to her chest.

Lance grabbed his son, hugging him close until Lochie wriggled and said, 'Daddy, it hurts.'

Poppy ran to the distraught woman, and Lance, on seeing Matt, gripped his shoulder. 'Thank you. Thank you for finding him, for finding us.'

Matt suggested Lance sit down. 'Actually, Lochie found us and your PLB is how we found you.'

Lance rubbed his head, relief clear in his eyes. 'One minute we could see him and the next he was gone. Then I lost our bearings searching for him because all this red rock looks the same.'

'I'm just glad you're safe.'

'Matt, I need the medical bag.' Poppy was crouched down next to the woman, who was pale and sweaty and had removed her shirt. 'Joanne fell on an outstretched arm and she's got a shoulder separation, but you've probably seen more of these than me.'

Matt introduced himself to the patient. 'I'm going to be as gentle as I can but this will probably hurt.'

Joanne flinched. 'It can't be worse than it already is, can it?'

Matt didn't want to promise anything. His fingers explored the top of the humerus and then followed the clavicle. A red tinge flushed the skin, indicating bleeding, and a distinctive bump marred the normally smooth line over the AC joint. 'I'm going to treat this with a cuff and collar sling and give you some strong painkillers to keep you comfortable on the long trip back to Bundallagong. We'll X-ray and ultrasound it when we arrive at the hospital and check for any other fractures, displacement, muscle and ligament damage. Does it hurt anywhere else?'

'Just our pride that we did something so ridiculously stupid.' Joanne leaned her head against Lance's shoulder as Lochie nestled between them. 'I'm never letting this child out of my sight again.'

'Good idea.'

Matt and Poppy spoke at the same time and he caught her vivid gaze full of intense feeling. For the briefest moment he experienced a moment of pure simpatico unlike anything he'd ever known.

Poppy pulled her theatre cap off her head and dropped it in the bin, wondering what on earth was going on in Bundallagong on this particular Thursday with two middle-of-the-night emergencies. She'd only just finished removing a lacerated spleen from a young man after a car accident when Matt's registrar, who was on night shift this week, had rushed up a guy with a bleeding gastric ulcer. It had been touch and go, with the patient bleeding so much that the blood bank was now in dire straits.

As she created a reminder on her phone to ring the radio station's breakfast show at seven to get the word out so Bundallagong residents would make a special effort to give blood today, she saw the time and sighed. 6:00 a.m. It was a really lousy time to finish as there was no point going home to sleep because she'd barely have got settled when she'd have to get up again. Yet she had ninety minutes to fill before she could do pre-surgical rounds. She thought of Matt; gorgeous and rumpled, sleeping spread-eagled across her bed. Even though she knew she wasn't going home right now, the fact he was there, in her bed, waiting for her, wound around her heart.

Careful. She gave herself a shake and walked quickly to her office.

She turned on her computer and brought up the email program as she did routinely every morning now, since Matt had pointedly said that bed was a work-free zone. She'd tried to argue that point but had deliciously lost, conceding defeat as he'd brought her to the brink of orgasm and then suggested he needed to stop right there to go and check his emails.

She'd even amazed herself by not sending William the surgical report this week. It had taken considerable strength of will and she'd almost capitulated, especially when her secretary had reminded her, but Matt's suggestion had been worth a try, given that everything else she'd tried hadn't made much difference in getting any response from her boss.

As thirty emails downloaded, the ping of her 'countdown' widget alerted her to the blinking number fourteen at the bottom of her screen. Ten weeks down and two weeks remaining in Bundallagong. Two weeks left with Matt.

The thought screamed through like a missile. *You'll miss him.*

'Ms Stanfield?'

She looked up distractedly, her brain stalled on how fast her time in Bundallagong had flown and how soon it would be over. One of the cleaners stood in the doorway of her office, and with wobbly legs she stood up and greeted him. 'Morning, Joe.'

He pulled a photo out of his overalls front pocket.

'My Louisa, she had the baby, and my son-in-law, he email me this.'

She'd been hearing about this long-awaited baby who'd been very slow to put in an appearance for ten days now, and as she stared down at the photo of a black-haired baby with fathomless eyes, her throat tightened. 'Congratulations, she's adorable.'

Joe beamed. 'Maria and I, we fly to Perth today to visit, but don't you worry. Franco will be looking after your office and I tell him to start your coffee at seven.'

A prickle of embarrassment made her feel uncomfortable. 'That's very kind, Joe, but, really, I can make my own coffee.'

The cleaner nodded as he put the photo back in his pocket. 'Yes, but if we look after you, perhaps you stay here in Bundallagong.'

Two and a half months ago Poppy would have scoffed at such a suggestion, but with every patient she'd treated, with every staff member she'd got to know and with every choir meeting, tiny roots had sprouted, connecting her to the community. She'd enjoyed her time here.

And if you don't get the job, would you stay?

The unexpected thought spun around her heart like the silky strands of a web, tying her to Bundallagong. Tying her to Matt.

A spasm hit, freezing her muscles, making it hard to breathe and hard to stand. Somehow she managed to smile, wish Joe a safe trip to Perth and sink back into her chair. She pushed her hands against her forehead and up into her hair.

No, no, no. You can't be that stupid.

Panic skittered through her, sending her reeling.

Falling for Matt, a man who still loved his dead wife, would be beyond dumb—it would be her worst nightmare. She sucked at relationships at the best of times but there was no way she could compete with Lisa, who'd been perfect alive and was now immortalised as a saint.

Have you learned nothing from your disastrous relationships? Her guiding Amazon rose up to her full height and brandished her sword and shield. *Woman up!*

Poppy pulled up memories of her father and Steven—betrayal, hurt, rejection—each recollection shoring up her resolve, but every time she thought of Matt she could only picture him laughing with her, teasing her, talking, listening and wrapping his arms around her each night until she fell into a deep sleep.

You love him.

Oh, God, no.

No, not love, please, not love. She dropped her head into her hands as the thought branded her with its full impact. She loved him. Little by little, day by day, she'd fallen in love with him so slowly she hadn't even realised it.

How had she left herself so unprotected?

She knew better than this. She knew from bitter experience that love wasn't enough and never had been. Love left a girl open to hurt and heartache, and to being let down in the worst way. Nothing good could ever come from being in love, and exploring this bit of self-realisation was pointless.

No promises, no regrets, no past and no future.

Matt's words rose up in her mind. She'd made a complete mess of something that should have been fun and short term. Once again, she'd let herself fall in love with a man who wasn't able to love her. She was too foolish for words.

Biting her lip, she welcomed the jolt of physical pain and rolled back her shoulders, pushing the feelings down deep to languish with the other relationship mistakes in her life and the ashes of her ill-fated marriage.

She tuned into work like she always did, keeping all her emotions at bay, and ploughed through the list of mail, deleting, forwarding and replying as required, while she sipped coffee and listened to the cacophony of sound that came with the dawn. She smiled as the sky filled with pink and grey as the native parrots rose from their sleep—another Bundallagong ritual she'd come to enjoy.

As she hit Send on the last email, her phone beeped its reminder. 7:00 a.m. She silenced it and immediately heard a ping from her computer, heralding a new email.

William.

A chill ran through her as her gut rolled on a wave of acid. She put her phone down and her hand hovered over the mouse for a few seconds before she moved the cursor over his name and clicked.

CHAPTER TEN

MATT woke with a start and stretched out to feel for
Poppy but his arm and hand only connected with cool
sheets. A vague memory slowly formed and he recalled
Poppy's phone ringing, her quietly murmured conversation, his grunted 'Do you need me?'

And her lips on his cheek as she'd said, 'Go back to
sleep.'

But now he was awake and the green light of the
bedside clock said 5:00 a.m. With a groan, he closed his
eyes and as his head hit the pillow he gratefully accepted
that at least it wasn't three. He hated 3:00 a.m., when
there was still so much night left and no more ability to
sleep. It became a long slog, waiting for the dawn, and
so as not to disturb Poppy, he'd get up and go and pace
the floors at his house.

His eyes shot open so abruptly that the muscles ached.
He hadn't woken up at 3:00 a.m. all this week. *It's been
longer than that.* He worked backwards and realised
with a start that he couldn't recall an early wake-up
since he'd told Poppy about Annie, and that had been
three weeks ago.

With a contented sigh, he rolled over, tugging at the
sheet, intending to grab one extra precious hour of sleep,

but his brain, already jolted awake, buzzed with ideas for the foundation. He accepted defeat, got up, walked into the pre-dawn chill—the only time Bundallagong was cool—and let himself into his house.

The long hallway echoed as he walked towards the kitchen and the house smelled musty, like it needed a good airing. He filled the kettle and then picked up the folder marked 'Lisa's Way', which he'd left on the table next to his laptop two nights ago. Grabbing a pen, he quickly scrawled down the name of Lisa's bead supplier that had been eluding him, along with some ideas to run past Sarah for a fundraising night at the neighbourhood centre. That done, he made coffee and set the plunger to rest on the top of the carafe while it brewed, and then opened the fridge for the milk.

A malodorous scent greeted him, the milk having become yoghurt and a lone lettuce now a ball of slime. He hastily dumped both in the bin and searched the pantry all the way to the back for some long-life milk. There was none. How could that be? He knew he was a poor shopper, but UHT milk was a staple that even in his darkest days he'd always had.

You're virtually living with Poppy.

The thought rocked him. He poured sugar into his coffee, stirring it fast as he grappled with his thoughts. Running back over the events of the last few weeks, the truth stared him in the face. He'd hardly been here. The reality was that he'd only been using his place to shower, change clothes, do laundry, and when Poppy was held up at work he'd come back here to do some foundation work.

Not even then.

He sat down hard in a chair as his legs trembled.

Last week he'd spent an evening at her place working on Lisa's Way while Poppy had been at choir practice because being over there was so much more pleasant than being here.

He heard the dawn thumping of Rupert but instead of being much-needed noise, he suddenly saw in his mind's eye the damage the reptile was likely inflicting on the roof. He looked around the room as if seeing it with new eyes, and for the first time the house didn't seem to be mocking him with its silence or its memories. He stood up and slowly walked the length and breadth of the house. Starting by opening the door to Annie's room, he systematically visited every other room in the house until he stood in the stripped-bare master bedroom. A room he'd avoided with the exception of the night Poppy had arrived.

He girded himself for the expected onslaught of pain, sadness and grief, the way it had been when he'd first arrived home from the Pacific, and the reason he'd moved to the guest room. But the house no longer spoke to him about loss—it didn't really speak to him at all.

Lisa and Annie were no longer part of the house.

The news should have broken his heart but instead it soothed it and an odd peace settled over him. His love for Lisa now resided in the creation of the foundation and his love for Annie poured into his work whenever he had scared and sick kids in the ED.

He ran his hand through his hair. He was no longer part of the house, either.

It's time.

He blew out a long breath laden with relief. He'd loved his wife and daughter dearly but now the time had come for him to move on with his life. Shoving his hands in his pockets, he glanced out the window at the house he'd come to think of as Poppy's place, despite the fact many people had lived in the house over the years.

Poppy.

Her lips matched her name and she was a bright spark of colour in what had been a very black time of his life. God, he enjoyed being with her. She made him laugh, she challenged him and at times frustrated the hell out of him, but she was the first person he thought of when he woke up in the morning and the last person he thought of when he closed his eyes at night.

That's love.

His chest tightened on his sharp intake of breath and he gripped the architrave. *Love.* The spasm faded, followed by a wave of warmth and the tendrils of belonging.

It *was* love.

He loved her.

He started to grin like a fool, his cheeks aching with happiness. She'd stormed into his life all attitude and vibrant energy and turned his grieving world upside down. Somewhere along the way he'd moved into her house and she'd moved into his heart. Now he couldn't imagine his life without her.

With a plan forming in his mind, he stepped out of the house and gently closed the door behind him.

Poppy stepped out of the theatre change rooms into the main hospital corridor and suddenly found herself being twirled around, pulled into strong arms and kissed so soundly her legs gave way.

Matt's sparkling brown eyes stared down at her as his fingers caressed her cheek. 'Hello.'

'Hel—' Her mouth stalled as her brain received the image from her eyes. Her hands flew to his hair, her fingers unaccountably aching as they tried unsuccessfully to lose themselves in the now short strands 'Oh. Your hair, it's...' She finally found her voice. 'You've had it cut.'

He grinned. 'I have. It was time.'

She'd always loved the way his hair reached his jaw-line, reminding her of a pirate. 'Why?'

But instead of replying, he just gave her a secret smile and pulled her into the on-call room and locked the door. A small white-cloth-covered table held a platter of freshly made sandwiches along with two bottles of fruit juice and a plate of what looked like peppermint slice. 'Lunch for two, courtesy of the kitchen.'

She smiled and kissed him, reminding herself of her plan to treasure every last moment with him. 'Lovely idea. I'm starving.' She greedily picked up a sandwich and started eating. 'Hmm, this is so good. Why haven't we done this before?'

'I guess we didn't have a reason to celebrate before.'

Her hand fell from her mouth and she stared at him in surprise. How did he know William had offered her the post of Chief of Surgery at Perth City? She hadn't told anyone. She'd read the email five times and had waited for the rush of joy that she'd finally got the job of her dreams, the one she'd been working towards for years. But instead of a rush it had been more of a slow trickle, as if she couldn't really believe she'd finally nailed it. But she had. The job was hers and the endpoint to her time in Bundallagong had arrived, as she'd always known it would. What hadn't arrived was the excitement she'd expected to experience on leaving the dust-filled town.

Matt stood in front her, his face full of warmth, friendship and pleasure for her, and the fact she'd achieved her long-held dream. Nothing about him showed that he was in any way sad about her leaving.

Why would you expect that? He still loves Lisa.

No promises, no regrets, no past and no future, remember?

But given all that, he'd thought to organise this lunch so they could celebrate now rather than waiting until the end of the day. No one had ever done anything like that for her before and she swallowed around the lump in her throat.

'Thank you.' She threw her arms around his neck with such enthusiasm that he staggered backwards, falling onto the bed. She lay against him and kissed him the way she knew made his head spin and his body hard.

He rolled her over. 'Had I known you were this easy to impress, I'd have done lunch a long time ago.' He stroked her hair. 'Marry me.'

Her gut went into freefall and she sat up fast, not able to believe what she thought she'd just heard. 'I beg your pardon?'

He sat up too, gently cupping her cheeks with his hands. 'Marry me.'

He knows about the job, he told you weeks ago you'd be great at it, and he still wants to marry you. Say yes.

But the question was so unexpected that she searched his face, his eyes, even the line of his mouth for clues.

Although everything seemed familiar, *nothing* was the same. A tremor of panic scuttled through her, mirroring her feelings early that morning when she'd realised she loved him. 'Are you sure you really want to marry me?'

'I do. I love you. I was floundering but you've changed everything and brought me back into the world. With you there's light.' His sincerity wrapped around her. 'I want to live with you until we're old and grey, and running around after ten grandchildren.'

Grandchildren. The aching longing that had been part of her since their day at the gorge surged and she let her head fall onto his shoulder, feeling the security of his breadth and the protection of his arms. *I love you.* The marvel of his words wove through her, tempting her with a promise of an amazing future. 'You see us with children?'

He kissed her hair. 'Why sound so surprised? You're great with kids and you'll be a sensational mother.'

She let the dream float over her and dared herself to believe. This wonderful man loved her and wanted to be the father of her children. *This time love and marriage will be different.* Her heart expanded, bursting open the self-imposed lock she'd chained to it years ago. 'We *will* be great parents.'

His lips touched hers with an almost reverent kiss, the touch imbued with a promise of things to come. 'Children are amazing and they change your life. I can picture a house, a garden, a deck, a pool. *Our* home.'

She could see it too and her hand pressed against his chest, feeling the beat of his heart. 'Somewhere by the river.'

His fingers played in her hair. 'I think you mean the beach.'

'No, I don't want to live in Fremantle because it's too far from the hospital. I suppose we could look at Cottlesloe if you think you'll miss the sea too much, but you might be surprised—the river's really pretty.' Still talking, she hugged him hard, excitement finally hitting her, bubbling through her like the bubbles of champagne. She had it all. It really was possible to have a man who loved her, a top job and in the future a family of her own.

'I wanted to tell you in person but somehow you found out and then you did this special and amazing thing for me and—' She stopped babbling, realising he'd gone completely still and was staring at her intently.

'What are you talking about?'

She joke-punched him on the arm. 'Don't be such a tease. You know exactly what I'm talking about.'

Confusion lay heavily on his cheeks and he shook his head slowly.

'But the celebration lunch...' And she realised the lunch wasn't connected with her new job at all but with his proposal. He didn't know her news. She grinned, loving how much pleasure it gave her to be the one to tell him as she'd originally planned. 'You're not only looking at your fiancée, you're also looking at Perth City's new Chief of Surgery.'

She opened her arms, expecting congratulations and an enormous embrace, but he just stared at her, his expression both stunned and surprised.

'You got the job?'

His words came out quietly without any acknowledgment of her massive achievement. The young Poppy

who'd always strived yet failed to impress her father
stirred deep inside her, sending out an aching ripple.
'William emailed me early this morning and followed
up with a phone call. The board has been really impressed by the work I've done, especially with the way
I had the full support of the staff.'

She reached out her hand, needing to touch him,
needing to see some sign from him that he was happy
for her. 'I couldn't have done it without your advice and
support.'

Finally he smiled and hugged her tightly before kissing her gently on the cheek. 'Congratulations, I'm so
proud of you.'

She breathed again, not realising she'd stopped.

His warm and loving gaze turned serious. 'But
now we're engaged, are you certain this is the job you
want?'

Every muscle in her body clenched. 'It's been everything I've worked towards for the last ten years.'

'Absolutely.' He nodded, his expression sincere. 'But
things have just changed, haven't they? It's best if we
live, work and raise our family here in Bundallagong.'

Steven's voice rose up like a spectre from the past,
taunting her with pain and bitter memories. *Poppy, we're
living at my place. It's really not up for discussion.*

When Annie arrived, Lisa and I moved back here.

Her heart quivered and her voice sounded overly
bright. 'So we just relocate and do it all in Perth instead.'

He frowned. 'We move to Perth and you take the
job?'

'Of course I take the job.' She smiled. 'Ten years, remember? All that hard work and now this is the reward. It's incredibly prestigious.'

He sighed, a long, low, ominous sound. 'In Bundallagong your surgical hours are almost workable, but how on earth are you going to balance family life with being Chief of Surgery?'

You're never home and I only asked you to do one thing—to collect my dry-cleaning and you couldn't even manage to do that.

It made you finish work a bit earlier.

Nobody has ever loved you without wanting to change you. First your father, then Steven and now Matt. A surge of anger obliterated her sob. She should have realised, she should have known this was all too good to be true. She should have recognised the massive signs from their conversation at Walker's Gorge.

She crossed her arms to stop herself from shaking. 'Worried you're going to have to learn how to shop and cook, are you?'

His jaw tightened. 'Believe me, cooking and shopping are the least of my concerns.'

Fool, fool, fool! He's no different. 'Oh, and let me guess what those concerns might be. You hate it that I won't be home every night before you, that I'll earn more than you, and that I'm not going to be barefoot and pregnant when you come home from a hard day at work.'

He threw up his hands. 'Now you're just being ridiculous.'

For heaven's sake, Poppy, you're my wife so act like one. Steven's voice faded as Matt's moved over it.

Lisa's choices made my life a lot easier. She remembered so clearly Matt saying that out at the water hole.

Her world tilted sideways, tipping out the fantasy of marriage and a family that she'd foolishly allowed herself to believe in for a few deluded moments. She so wanted to trust that he loved her for who she was but, like her father and Steven, he could only love her if she changed for him. If she gave up everything for him. Her chest tightened so much she could barely breathe as the past choked her.

Matt didn't really love her, he just thought he did. He only wanted a replacement for Lisa. His love, just like that of the men before him, came with conditions that would destroy them both. She stood up, moving away from him, and forced herself to do what she should have done the moment he'd proposed.

'I can't marry you, Matt. I can't make your life easier by being a stay-at-home wife. I can't be Lisa's replacement and live in the same house and help you live the life you had with her.'

Poppy's words plunged into Matt's heart like a knife, leaving him completely bewildered. 'God, Poppy, this has *nothing* to do with Lisa.' But he could tell by the look on her face she didn't believe him.

He tried to explain it. 'Lisa *chose* to stay at home and I supported her in doing that. I'm not asking you to give up working—of course you need to work. I want you to work. All I'm asking is that we live and work *here* so we can protect what we have.'

The starchy Poppy he hadn't seen in weeks materialised, her voice sharp and brisk. 'What we *have* is a short-term affair with an end date. We've been in this sensual bubble where it's just been us and the sex, but that isn't real life.' Her hand touched her pendant. 'Today real life intruded and already it's tearing us apart and it's only going to get worse.'

'It doesn't have to.' He walked towards her, wanting to touch her, wanting to remind her that what they had was worth saving. 'I'd consider moving to Perth if you took another job there. Look, if we compromise, we can make this work.'

Her eyes flashed. 'Not when one of us wants something at the expense of the other.'

'I'm not stopping you being a surgeon!' Trying to rein in his frustration, he ploughed his hand through his hair, only to discover with a shock just how unsatisfying it was with short hair. 'Give me some credit here, Poppy. I know how much time it takes to make a relationship work and if you become Chief of Surgery, you'll disappear into that job and it will kill us.'

She shook her head, her lips compressed into a thin line. 'Obviously I can't be married to you and be the surgeon I want to be.'

His heart slammed against his ribcage and slithered down, a bleeding, battered mess. 'You really believe that? You're going to walk away from this amazing thing we share for a job?'

'A job?' Her eyes glittered with a collage of emotions that swirled together with no defined edges. 'You really don't get it at all.'

Anger born of desperate hurt spewed bile. 'Oh, I get it. I get it loud and clear. My God, I thought you'd grown while you were here. I thought you'd worked out what was important in life, that it was people and relationships and love that counted, not pushing yourself to win at any cost. You're putting this job ahead of everything else. You really don't have a clue, do you?'

She tilted her chin up, her eyes flashing and her shoulders sharp, reminding him of the very first time he'd met her. 'I have more of a clue than you do, Matt. This conversation is just the start of what will happen to us if we get married, and the arguments will only get worse until we're tearing each other apart and wondering why the hell we once thought we loved each other. I'm doing this for us.'

'That's total garbage, Poppy. You're doing it for yourself and I only hope being Chief of Surgery keeps you warm at night.'

She flinched. 'I think we're done now. Goodbye, Matt.'

The door slammed behind her, shattering his hopes and dreams and leaving him devastated and alone.

CHAPTER ELEVEN

'MAIL for you, Ms Stanfield.'

Poppy glanced up from her spreadsheet to see the Perth City internal postwoman holding out a sheaf of mail. 'Thanks, Leanne. By the way, how did that biology assignment go?'

Surprise raced across the young woman's face before she smiled shyly. 'Wow, I can't believe you remembered that I was doing the course. I got an A.'

Poppy smiled as she picked up her outbound mail from the tray. 'Of course I remembered. It sounds like you're well on the way to getting the mark you need to get into nursing.'

'Hope so.' Leanne took the proffered mail. 'See ya, Ms Stanfield.'

'Bye, Leanne.'

As she walked out, William walked in, clutching a manila folder. 'First-name terms with the clerks, Poppy?' His brows rose. 'What the hell happened to you in that godforsaken place?'

'And hello to you too, William.' She pasted a smile on her face for her acerbic boss. 'Perhaps you should visit Bundallagong one day.'

He either missed or ignored the jibe. 'Harrumph. Far too busy for that and so are you.'

He wasn't wrong. She'd thought her first two weeks in Bundallagong had been long and arduous but they'd been almost relaxed in comparison to her start at Perth City. Not that she minded working hard, she didn't, which given her current circumstances was a good thing. But unlike in the past, when work had excited her, now a lot of it seemed like a chore.

When she'd first arrived back in Perth she hadn't cared how busy she was because work had filled her brain to capacity, leaving no space to think about Bundallagong, Matt and heartache. But just recently, when most nights she was only home for barely enough time to sleep, she'd started to think William's expectations of his department heads might be excessive. For the first time in her life she was pining to sit on her couch and just 'be'. Yesterday afternoon she'd even found herself wondering who she knew in Perth who might want to catch up for a drink and a chat, and much to her surprise she'd checked the notice-board for any posters about product parties. *You're lonely.*

William dropped the file on her desk. 'Applications for the surgical registrars and consultant operating rights. You also have to pick someone to go to Bundallagong next month. Interviews start at seven on Thursday evening. Happy reading.'

She stifled a groan. She'd been determined to have one night at home reading this week but job applications didn't count. 'I can't do Thursday.'

He fired her one of his penetrating looks. 'You *are* full of surprises today. I thought your life was the hospital but don't tell me you actually have a private life?'

She bristled, even though he was pretty much correct. 'I've organised a movie night fundraiser in the hospital auditorium for that night. I can interview earlier in the day.'

'Oh, yes, I think I saw a poster about that—something to do with women in Samoa? Can't you just do your speech at the start and then leave?'

Somehow she held onto her temper. 'No, William, I can't. I need to be there, sell raffle tickets, answer questions and thank people for their support.'

He nodded slowly, as if absorbing the news. 'I'll get my secretary to contact you with the new interview date but, Poppy, next time you act out of character, let me know.'

Quietly seething, she watched his retreating back and pictured daggers. Just because she wanted to have *one* night off, it didn't mean she'd changed.

You never got involved in anything out of work before Bundallagong.

True, but just because she was raising money for a worthy cause, it didn't mean she'd changed. *Lisa's Way is not just any worthy cause, though, is it? You're doing it to feel close to Matt.*

Blocking the perceptive voice in her head and throwing off her William-induced ill humour, she started flicking through her mail and her hand stalled on a small square box. She sliced open the tape with her letter knife and drew out a CD and a card written in Sarah's bold script.

Hi! Wanted you to have the first copy of the choir's CD, recorded at the concert! Sorry it's taken this long to get it into the mail! Choir's going great and Jen's conducting. Justin and I in Perth 8th-9th for a childless weekend, but can't have sex all the time ;-) so can you do Sunday brunch?

Poppy laughed as she read the words, able to hear Sarah's voice in her head, and a fizz of anticipation bubbled inside her at the thought of seeing her. They'd shared some laughs at choir, the pub and at their respective houses and it would be wonderful to kick back over a leisurely brunch and hear all the Bundallagong news.

Matt sold his house and is in Samoa doing work for Lisa's Way. Still no replacement surgeon here and we miss your bossy but motivating ways.

A leaden feeling settled in her belly, overriding the excitement. She hadn't done anything fun since she'd got back to Perth. With shocked surprise, she realised exactly how much she missed Sarah and Jen's company.
You miss Matt.
You know you miss Matt. Every. Single. Day.
A fresh wave of pain washed through her. *Call him.*
The idea had her reaching for the phone but as her fingers started dialling she dropped the handset back into the cradle like it was on fire. Exactly what was she going to say? 'I miss you.' But then what? Nothing had altered; the impasse still stood. At least this time she'd found out before getting married that the man she loved wanted to change her.
So why are you so miserable?

Distracting herself, she shoved the choir's CD into her computer and while it loaded she read the last bit of the note.

Hope Perth is worth it. Sarah xx

She pushed the note aside and then pulled it back, her gaze fixated on five words. *Hope Perth is worth it.*

Deep in the recesses of her mind a small voice asked a question. *Are you sure this job is what you want?* The question scared her witless and she stomped on it hard and fast. *Of course it's what I want. I can depend on it.*

OK, if you think so. But the reply didn't sound all that convincing.

The CD finally started playing and her throat tightened as the choir's voices filled the air. She closed her eyes and Bundallagong moved into the office. She could smell the dust and the salt, see the smiling faces of her staff, visualise the old choir hall and feel the camaraderie of the women. She heard the pride in their voices and she knew how much more than just music the choir meant to its members; how much it had come to mean to her. An aching lethargy came over her, dragging at every muscle like flu. She ached for the connection she'd shared with the women.

You ache for Matt.

And she couldn't deny it. She pictured him lying in her bed with his arms around her, sitting at the kitchen bench, listening to her talk about her day and offering advice, and laughing as they swung Lochie between them.

But he wanted you to give up something that was

vitally important to you. She bit her lips to stop tears spilling. She loved him but, like her father and Steven, he just didn't love her enough.

Get fresh air and coffee. Coffee will help. She pushed back her chair and left her office, walking across the road to the park and the coffee vendor. Families sat under trees, having picnics, and children on school holidays charged around kicking footballs.

She joined the queue, enjoying the sunshine on her skin after too many weeks of being inside. *You saw more of the outside world in Bundallagong.*

Yeah, red-dust dirt.

Walker's Gorge was red dust and dirt but it had a rugged beauty.

'Poppy, good to see you.'

With a start she pulled her attention away from memories of Bundallagong to the present, and the outstretched hand in front of her. 'Oh, Alistair, you're still in Perth?'

She'd met Alistair Roland once, soon after she'd returned, and she'd assumed he'd gone back east. 'Sorry, obviously you're here and not in Sydney.'

He laughed. 'We moved to Perth lock, stock and barrel five months ago. So, how's the new job and workaholic William treating you?'

She scanned his face, looking for signs of resentment that she'd got the job over him, but all she could see was genuine interest. She thought about the punishing hours. 'You know, like any new job, it takes a while to get a handle on it.'

'The surgery's the easy bit, right?'

She blinked at his insight and relaxed. 'I have days I

want to hide in Theatre and not come out in case there's another manila folder on my desk.'

He nodded in understanding. 'You're lucky you're single.'

Irritation and sadness buffeted her. 'Why do you say that?'

A boy ran over. Alistair stretched out his arm and the boy snuggled in against him. 'Hey, Dad, can I have a strawberry smoothie?'

'Sure.'

'Thanks.' The boy tore off again.

Alistair shook his head, his expression full of affection. 'That streak was Jake and...' he pointed to another boy chasing a football '...that's Lucas. My wife Deanna is reading under the tree. They came down to meet me for lunch because I had a cancellation, and that's the beauty of Perth over Sydney. Lifestyle.'

'Exactly.' This was what she and Matt could have had if he'd been prepared to leave Bundallagong. 'It's just what I was trying to explain to someone not that long ago and it's great you've been doing this sort of thing since you arrived.'

A light frown creased his forehead. 'The whole time I was working for William, I hardly saw the boys.'

'Oh, why was that?'

'Seriously? You're working for William as Chief of Surgery and you're asking me that? How many evenings have you been home since you became Chief?'

None.

But that's because I want to be busy.

Not totally.

Alistair nodded, taking her silence as an answer. 'Which is why that job defeated the point of us moving here. Deanna's amazing but she didn't marry me to become a sole parent and that's what was happening. I want to be involved in my kids' lives.' Passion and love shone on his face. 'The stress of trying to do the job and be a dad and a husband, well, it was crazy stuff so I pulled out of the running. Only a single surgeon can do that job.'

She stared at him, stunned. 'Wasn't it hard to walk away from the sort of job you spent your entire career aiming for?'

He gave a wry smile. 'You know, I really thought it would be, but at the end of the day I realised you can't have the one hundred per cent best career and a real family. So I'm not Chief but I get to see my kids most evenings. It's all about balance.'

If we go to Perth you'll disappear into that job and it will kill us.

Her gut rolled with nausea and she almost gagged. Alistair Roland with a supportive stay-at-home wife had walked away from the top job to protect his family.

'Poppy, are you OK?' Alistair looked concerned.

She tried to rally as her head swirled with thoughts and she managed a sort-of smile. 'Nothing a coffee won't fix. So what are you doing job-wise now?'

He moved up with the queue. 'It's been a huge step but I've gone into private practice and it's giving me the flexibility with the boys I could never have as Chief of Surgery. Being a parent is one big juggling act and I guess it's always going to be a work-in-progress but Southgate's given me operating rights and I'm really hoping you'll approve my application for City.'

Somehow she managed to nod, give her assurances that she would support his application and then finished the conversation with a promise of meeting his wife at a later date. Somehow her legs carried her back across the park to the reflection room at the hospital. In the cool quiet of the sanctuary, her heart thundered loudly and her stomach sizzled with acid that spilled into her throat.

Give me some credit, Poppy. I know how much time it takes to make a relationship work.

But she hadn't, she hadn't given Matt any credit at all. She'd seen his love and care for them as a couple as a direct attack on herself, and had lumped him in with her father and Steven. But Matt was nothing like them. He hadn't been trying to change her. Not wanting her to take this job hadn't been lack of support at all. He'd been trying to create the opportunity so they could try and have it all—love, marriage, career and a family. And she'd let her past control her and had completely messed it up.

Her head fell into her hands as everything she'd thought she believed in came crashing down around her. She'd risen to the top of her career ladder in the job of her dreams and she had absolutely nothing else. Five months ago it wouldn't have mattered that work was all she had, but William was right. She'd changed. Bundallagong had changed her. Matt had changed her. Being Chief of Surgery was no longer enough.

She wanted more.

She wanted Matt.

She'd put her trust in the wrong basket and made the most horrendous mistake of her life. She'd been so deluded, so busy playing the blame game, but it was all her own fault she was alone and miserable—she'd brought it on herself.

So stop whining and do something about it.

For the first time ever, her father's words actually helped.

She pulled out her phone and hesitated. She might be risking everything for nothing.

Just do it. Deal with any regrets later.

Matt sat contemplatively in the airport lounge at Perth airport. His flight from Apia had been late, making him miss his connection to Bundallagong, and now his only option was to sit out the two hours until the next flight. He texted the new flight details to Sarah, who was now on the Lisa's Way board, explaining his delay, and then let out a long sigh. The funny thing about travel was that the moment the date for returning arrived, the brain raced ahead and took up residence at home while the body still had to undertake the journey.

Home. He shifted in his chair. He didn't actually have one.

He'd sold the Bundallagong house fully furnished, as he'd planned to do before he'd proposed to Poppy, and had stowed a few boxes in storage before heading to Samoa to set up Lisa's Way. Two months later, with a fantastic young woman on the ground in the village, and the connections in Australia all set up it was time to go back to Bundallagong or even think of working somewhere else.

Perhaps he'd look at the jobs online while he was waiting but first he'd finish up his Lisa's Way financial report. Using the wireless internet in the lounge, he checked the foundation's bank balance and saw with pleasant surprise a new and sizeable deposit. He read the transfer note. Stanfield PCFR.

Poppy.

Stunned to see her name, he stared at the cryptic PCFR, trying hard to work out what the other four letters meant. His brain finally clicked in. Perth City Fund Raiser.

His heart beat faster. He couldn't believe that despite everything, despite how much she'd hurt him and the harsh way they'd parted, Poppy had organised a fundraiser.

Did it mean anything?

His wounded heart said, *No. Don't even go there.*

He ordered a coffee and a Danish pastry then turned his attention back to the financial statement and the rows of figures.

'Here's your coffee.'

Thinking that being in Perth was really doing his head in because the voice sounded just like Poppy's, he looked up abruptly. Ice and heat tore through him as his gaze met those unforgettable vivid blue eyes.

'Hello, Matt.'

She handed him a coffee and he noticed she held a cup, too. A thousand thoughts sprinted though his head but his anger won, coming out as sarcasm. 'It's a Wednesday morning. I would have thought you'd be at work.'

She shuddered slightly and he watched the movement roll down her body. *Irreconcilable differences.* He didn't regret for a moment that he'd just highlighted the reason they'd parted so acrimoniously. If she thought she could just sit down and 'chat' like old friends, she was wrong. Very wrong.

He caught sight of a familiar red suitcase and things fell into place. 'Ah, it's conference season.'

'Here's your pastry, sir. Sorry for the delay.' The smiling attendant put down a plate and looked at Poppy. 'I brought you one as well as a thank-you for helping me out back there with the coffee disaster.'

Poppy smiled warmly. 'No problem.'

As the attendant walked away, Poppy turned back to Matt, her hand creeping towards the silver P. Half of him wanted to pull her hard against him but the other half demanded he stay cool and aloof so that there was no danger of his heart ever being battered by her again.

'Can I sit down?'

He shrugged. 'Suit yourself.'

She sank onto the couch and crossed her long legs. 'Sarah said you've been in Samoa.'

Her perfume enveloped him, threatening to take him back to a time when he'd thought they'd be together for ever. He fought the memory by flicking the collar on his shirt. 'Two months. I'm on my way back to Bundallagong.'

'How's Lisa's Way going?'

He sighed. 'Poppy, do you really want to make polite chitchat?'

She rolled her lips inwards. 'I'm enquiring about it because I'm a contributor and a friend.'

'You're a *contributor*.'

She flinched at the harshness in his voice but he didn't care. Did she really think she could sit there next to him in her tailored black suit and pretend they hadn't shared anything? Did she think he'd overlook the fact that she'd put a job ahead of everything? A job she'd left him for?

The black heart of his pain spluttered.

She gave a grim smile. 'Matt, I don't—'

He held up a hand. 'I don't want to argue, either. I don't think I even want to talk to you. I'm not going to ask you how the job's going because I'm not interested.'

She breathed in, seeming to hold her breath. 'I've quit.'

Shock made him gape. 'You've what?'

'I've quit and I have a new job.'

His gaze returned to her red suitcase and he immediately recalled the prestigious job he'd seen advertised soon after she'd left. It carried more kudos than the job she had, and Poppy didn't like to lose. He couldn't keep the bitterness out of his voice. 'Ah. St Stephen's in Sydney. Of course, that makes total sense.' He couldn't bring himself to offer congratulations.

'Ah, no, not St Stephen's.' She twisted her hands in her lap in an unusual display of unease. 'The last decision I made as Chief of Surgery was to appoint a permanent surgeon to meet the needs of the growing population of Bundallagong. I have firsthand experience of how much one is needed.'

Every word she spoke reminded him of what they'd lost and he struggled to sound enthusiastic. 'Well, that's good news for the town. Who is it?'

'I'm the new surgeon in Bundallagong.'

Her words slammed into him and a glimmer of hope sprouted in a sea of pain, but the memory of how much she'd hurt him made it struggle.

Poppy watched Matt, knowing this was the moment of truth, and it petrified her. Everything about him, from the strands of his long hair to the tips of toes shod in leather boat shoes, emanated anger. Had she really been so naive as to think he'd welcome her with open arms?

You hurt him so much. From the moment she'd got Sarah's text telling her Matt was in the airport lounge, and from the second she'd seen him, she'd wanted to throw her arms around his neck and tell him what a fool she'd been and beg for his forgiveness. But she had to do it this way and now she was dying inside, waiting for him to speak.

He sat perfectly still, his body almost as rigid as a statue, and the only movement was the complex map of emotions on his face, with hurt shining the brightest. When he finally spoke his voice sounded strained. 'Why?'

She swallowed hard, knowing this conversation was never going to be easy, and tried a touch of levity. 'Because Bundallagong needs a kick-ass surgeon.'

Not even a hint of a smile hovered on his lips but his eyes sought hers. 'Is there another reason?'

This time she went for honesty. 'Yes. I love you.'

A flicker of something flared in his eyes and faded. 'You once said you loved me but you left me, putting a job ahead of us.'

She swallowed against the lump in her throat. 'I know and I'm sorry. I got it all horribly wrong.'

'Yeah, you did.'

His ice-cool voice made her heart hammer hard against her ribs, and she could hear the tremble in her voice but she knew she was fighting for the most important 'job' of her life. 'I was scared. I thought you were trying to make me a different person, just like my father and Steven, trying to make me more like Lisa, and my fear got in the way. I let it screw everything up.' Her hands twisted together. 'I now know you weren't trying to change me. You were making sure we'd make it by creating a wonderful life for us. You saw what I couldn't see, that being Chief of Surgery would consume me and destroy us.'

His expression gave nothing away. 'And yet you didn't believe me. Exactly when did you work this out?'

His quiet but drilling words made her sweat and she pressed her damp palms against her black skirt. Everything she held dear rode on her explanation. 'I missed you every day like a part of me had been lost.'

His jaw tensed. 'I find that hard to believe. You didn't even call.'

The accusation stung but she wore the pain like a badge. 'I know. I've made a mess of everything. When I first came back to Perth I thought I was returning to my life, slipping back into a familiar and secure groove. But it didn't feel right, and it isn't a life I want any more.'

She gulped in a breath and pushed on, exposing her heart like she'd never exposed it before. 'I came to Bundallagong thinking it was a waste of my time, but without me realising, it changed my life. *You* changed my life. I'd always believed that work kept me safe and gave me everything I needed but then I met you. You opened up my world, showed me that life is to be lived, not hidden from. No job, no matter how much I sacrificed to get it, is worth it if I lose you.'

He swallowed hard and his voice wavered. 'The Poppy I met when she first arrived in Bundallagong would never have admitted she was wrong but I need to ask you one thing. Are you absolutely certain this is what you want?'

She nodded. 'It's what I want most in the world. I want to be a surgeon, not an administrator. I want time with friends and girls' nights out. I want a family, but most of all I want you.'

Extending her hand, she let it hover between them. Trying to hold back tears, she sent up the wish of her life. 'I know I need to prove to you that I've changed, and I know at times I can be difficult and that I'm nothing like Lisa, but I need to ask you one thing. Do you want me?'

Matt's fingers bypassed her hand and cupped her cheek. 'Lisa was the love of my boyhood and what we shared will always be part of me but, Poppy, *you're* the love of my manhood. You're my future.'

She fell apart, tears streaming down her face. He pulled her into his arms, burying his face in her hair. 'I want you because you're you. Passionate, giving and full of wonderful flaws, just like me.'

She sniffed. 'I can be stubborn with workaholic tendencies but I'm working on that. I'm going to block out non-work time in the week and stick to it, plus having a new surgical registrar is going to help.'

Surprise lit his face and he grinned. 'The last chief of surgery at Perth City *was* very proactive for Bundallagong.'

She laughed. 'Someone has to look out for rural communities.'

He stroked her hair. 'I hate shopping and housework and I can't cook, but I'll pay Lizzie to keep the freezer full of healthy meals and I'll grill on the weekends.'

She snuggled in against him, pressing her hand against his heart. 'Who's cleaning the house?'

'Mrs Ferguson.'

'I can live with that.'

'And I can't wait to live with you.' He smiled, his face

radiating love. 'So you'll want a year in the job before we start a family?'

Her heart swelled with so much love and adoration that it almost burst. He'd always known work was important to her and he still did, and she couldn't believe how she'd almost lost him. 'You're forgetting I've already had three months in the position and with an experienced registrar starting next week I think he'll be able to fly solo in about nine months.'

The delight on his face mirrored her own. 'I can't wait to start practising.'

'Will you marry me, Matt Albright?'

'I most certainly will, Poppy Stanfield.'

She grinned and ran her fingers through his hair. 'How do you feel about keeping this longer?'

His eyes took on a familiar smoky hue that made her weak with longing. 'Ms Stanfield, do you have a thing for guys with long hair?'

'No, just for you.'

He cupped her face and kissed her long and hard, his lips infusing her with his love, support, caring and passion.

'Passengers on Flight 273 to Bundallagong, your flight is boarding now. Please make your way to gate seventeen.'

Matt stood up and extended his hand. 'Let's go home.'

Home.

To the red dust of Bundallagong with the man she loved. She couldn't wait.

AUGUST 2011
HARDBACK TITLES

ROMANCE

Bride for Real	Lynne Graham
From Dirt to Diamonds	Julia James
The Thorn in His Side	Kim Lawrence
Fiancée for One Night	Trish Morey
The Untamed Argentinian	Susan Stephens
After the Greek Affair	Chantelle Shaw
The Highest Price to Pay	Maisey Yates
Under the Brazilian Sun	Catherine George
There's Something About a Rebel...	Anne Oliver
The Crown Affair	Lucy King
Australia's Maverick Millionaire	Margaret Way
Rescued by the Brooding Tycoon	Lucy Gordon
Not-So-Perfect Princess	Melissa McClone
The Heart of a Hero	Barbara Wallace
Swept Off Her Stilettos	Fiona Harper
Mr Right There All Along	Jackie Braun
The Tortured Rebel	Alison Roberts
Dating Dr Delicious	Laura Iding

HISTORICAL

Married to a Stranger	Louise Allen
A Dark and Brooding Gentleman	Margaret McPhee
Seducing Miss Lockwood	Helen Dickson
The Highlander's Return	Marguerite Kaye

MEDICAL™

The Doctor's Reason to Stay	Dianne Drake
Career Girl in the Country	Fiona Lowe
Wedding on the Baby Ward	Lucy Clark
Special Care Baby Miracle	Lucy Clark

AUGUST 2011 LARGE PRINT TITLES

ROMANCE

Jess's Promise	Lynne Graham
Not For Sale	Sandra Marton
After Their Vows	Michelle Reid
A Spanish Awakening	Kim Lawrence
In the Australian Billionaire's Arms	Margaret Way
Abby and the Bachelor Cop	Marion Lennox
Misty and the Single Dad	Marion Lennox
Daycare Mum to Wife	Jennie Adams

HISTORICAL

Miss in a Man's World	Anne Ashley
Captain Corcoran's Hoyden Bride	Annie Burrows
His Counterfeit Condesa	Joanna Fulford
Rebellious Rake, Innocent Governess	Elizabeth Beacon

MEDICAL™

Cedar Bluff's Most Eligible Bachelor	Laura Iding
Doctor: Diamond in the Rough	Lucy Clark
Becoming Dr Bellini's Bride	Joanna Neil
Midwife, Mother...Italian's Wife	Fiona McArthur
St Piran's: Daredevil, Doctor...Dad!	Anne Fraser
Single Dad's Triple Trouble	Fiona Lowe

SEPTEMBER 2011
HARDBACK TITLES

ROMANCE

The Kanellis Scandal	Michelle Reid
Monarch of the Sands	Sharon Kendrick
One Night in the Orient	Robyn Donald
His Poor Little Rich Girl	Melanie Milburne
The Sultan's Choice	Abby Green
The Return of the Stranger	Kate Walker
Girl in the Bedouin Tent	Annie West
Once Touched, Never Forgotten	Natasha Tate
Nice Girls Finish Last	Natalie Anderson
The Italian Next Door...	Anna Cleary
From Daredevil to Devoted Daddy	Barbara McMahon
Little Cowgirl Needs a Mum	Patricia Thayer
To Wed a Rancher	Myrna Mackenzie
Once Upon a Time in Tarrula	Jennie Adams
The Secret Princess	Jessica Hart
Blind Date Rivals	Nina Harrington
Cort Mason – Dr Delectable	Carol Marinelli
Survival Guide to Dating Your Boss	Fiona McArthur

HISTORICAL

The Lady Gambles	Carole Mortimer
Lady Rosabella's Ruse	Ann Lethbridge
The Viscount's Scandalous Return	Anne Ashley
The Viking's Touch	Joanna Fulford

MEDICAL ROMANCE™

Return of the Maverick	Sue MacKay
It Started with a Pregnancy	Scarlet Wilson
Italian Doctor, No Strings Attached	Kate Hardy
Miracle Times Two	Josie Metcalfe

0811 Gen Std LP

SEPTEMBER 2011
LARGE PRINT TITLES

ROMANCE

Too Proud to be Bought	Sharon Kendrick
A Dark Sicilian Secret	Jane Porter
Prince of Scandal	Annie West
The Beautiful Widow	Helen Brooks
Rancher's Twins: Mum Needed	Barbara Hannay
The Baby Project	Susan Meier
Second Chance Baby	Susan Meier
Her Moment in the Spotlight	Nina Harrington

HISTORICAL

More Than a Mistress	Ann Lethbridge
The Return of Lord Conistone	Lucy Ashford
Sir Ashley's Mettlesome Match	Mary Nichols
The Conqueror's Lady	Terri Brisbin

MEDICAL ROMANCE™

Summer Seaside Wedding	Abigail Gordon
Reunited: A Miracle Marriage	Judy Campbell
The Man with the Locked Away Heart	Melanie Milburne
Socialite...or Nurse in a Million?	Molly Evans
St Piran's: The Brooding Heart Surgeon	Alison Roberts
Playboy Doctor to Doting Dad	Sue MacKay